"Look at me," Jax urged, breaking the smoldering silence.

And Lucy looked even though she knew she shouldn't, desire clawing at her insides, awakening the yearning buried deep within her body. A ragged breath escaped her, her pulse racing.

"We're getting married as soon as it can be arranged," Jax decreed.

Her head flew up. "You can't just—"

"We do it for Bella. Together we make a family," Jax intoned.

"Do you really *want* to do this?" Lucy whispered shakily.

"I want you. I want my daughter. To give her what we both want, to give her what she *deserves*, we have to get married. We will fight," Jax forecast. "But we're good at making up again."

Lucy flushed and nodded jerkily and he laughed huskily for they had always ended up in bed after arguments, taking refuge in the sexual unity that bridged their differences.

"You say the craziest things," Lucy muttered, shaking her head while locked to the stunning green eyes gleaming below his black lashes.

"I will say whatever I have to say to get that ring on your finger," Jax admitted truthfully. "The world's your oyster tonight, *koukla mou*."

Brides for the Taking

With this ring...

On their mother's deathbed, Polly and Ellie Dixon
are both given a name, a ring and the news of
a half sister they've never met!

The search for their heritage leads these
three sisters into the paths of three incredible
alpha males...and it's not long before they're
walking down the aisle!

Don't miss this fabulous trilogy,
starting with Polly's story...

The Desert King's Blackmailed Bride
February 2017

Continuing with Ellie's story

The Italian's One-Night Baby
April 2017

Finishing with Lucy's story

Sold for the Greek's Heir
June 2017

Lynne Graham

SOLD FOR THE GREEK'S HEIR

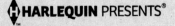

Recycling programs
for this product may
not exist in your area.

ISBN-13: 978-0-373-06069-6

Sold for the Greek's Heir

First North American Publication 2017

Copyright © 2017 by Lynne Graham

Printed in U.S.A.

Lynne Graham was born in Northern Ireland and has been a keen romance reader since her teens. She is very happily married to an understanding husband who has learned to cook since she started to write! Her five children keep her on her toes. She has a very large dog who knocks everything over, a very small terrier who barks a lot and two cats. When time allows, Lynne is a keen gardener.

Books by Lynne Graham

Harlequin Presents

Bought for the Greek's Revenge
The Sicilian's Stolen Son
Leonetti's Housekeeper Bride
The Secret His Mistress Carried
The Dimitrakos Proposition

Brides for the Taking

The Desert King's Blackmailed Bride
The Italian's One-Night Baby

Christmas with a Tycoon

The Italian's Christmas Child
The Greek's Christmas Bride

The Notorious Greeks

The Greek Demands His Heir
The Greek Commands His Mistress

Bound by Gold

The Billionaire's Bridal Bargain
The Sheikh's Secret Babies

The Legacies of Powerful Men

Ravelli's Defiant Bride
Christakis's Rebellious Wife
Zarif's Convenient Queen

Visit the Author Profile page at Harlequin.com for more titles.

For Rachel and Michael for their unswerving
support and their ability to consider my characters
as seriously as I do.

CHAPTER ONE

IN THE PIT, Jax Antonakos climbed out of the low-slung car, adrenalin still pumping fiercely from the excitement of the race. Only a show race for charity, though, he reminded himself wryly, bracing himself as he was engulfed by a large, noisy crowd of people.

He yanked off his helmet, revealing tousled black hair and eyes as strikingly green as emeralds, and the usual collective female gasp of appreciation sounded. While he stripped off his track regalia, photographers flashed cameras, journalists demanded quotes and shot questions at him and beautiful women tried to sidle closer to him, but then all of that was the norm in Jax's goldfish bowl of a world.

Jax, however, ignored all of them to stride over and congratulate the winner of the race and the reigning world champion.

'You gave me a good run for a man who hasn't been behind a wheel in years!' Dirk conceded cheer-

fully. 'Maybe you shouldn't be pushing numbers behind a desk, maybe you should still be racing.'

'No, Jax is a business genius,' a female voice
crowed from Jax's other side, and before he could
react the bubbly brunette wrapped her arms round
him with enthusiasm. 'Thank you so much for stepping in last minute to do this when Stefan had to let
me down. You know how grateful I am.'

'Kat,' Jax acknowledged, frowning as the photographers predictably went for a shot of them as a
couple. But he and Kat Valtinos weren't a couple,
no matter how much the media and their families
wanted them to be, both of them being conveniently
young, single and very rich.

Jax stepped back from Kat with a guarded smile.
He liked Kat, he had *always* liked her but his father
was in for a disappointment if he was still hoping
for a dynastic marriage that would unite their parents' massive business empires. Unfortunately the
photos would only encourage him in that delusion.

'Let's get you a drink,' Kat urged, closing a possessive arm round his spine. 'I really appreciate you
flying out here and doing this for me today at such
short notice—'

'It was for a good cause,' Jax pointed out. 'And
you're a friend—'

'A friend who could be *so* much more,' Kat whispered with laden intent in his ear.

'I enjoyed the race,' Jax admitted, choosing to be

tactful and sidestep her leading comment. After all, there was no kind way of telling her *why* she was wasting her time chasing him and, with his reputation for womanising, it would be sheer hypocrisy for him to do so. Even now he retained fond memories of Kat's raunchy wildness when they were teenagers and he had been on the outskirts of the same social set but he still wasn't willing to marry a woman who had slept with every one of his friends. If that was a double standard, so be it, he acknowledged grimly.

In any case, he didn't want a wife, *any* kind of wife. Nor was he prepared to deliver the grandchildren his father, Heracles Antonakos, was so eager to have. Parenting was a minefield: Jax knew that better than anyone because he had stumbled through his own very unhappy childhood, filled as it had been with constant change and even more constant emotional drama.

His parents had gone through a bitter divorce when he was only a toddler and for the following twenty-five years his father had pretty much ignored his younger son's existence. Heracles's elder son, Argo, had been born from his first marriage. Widowed, Heracles had plunged into his second marriage far too quickly and he had never forgiven his second wife, Jax's mother, for her subsequent infidelity. Jax had paid the price for his mother's extramarital affair in more ways than one. He had had no safe harbour from which to escape the fallout of his mother's broken relationships, nor any paternal support. He had struggled alone through Mariana's divorces, suicide attempts and regular stays in rehabilitation facilities.

And one of his earliest memories was of hiding in terror in a cupboard from one of his mother's druggie meltdowns. He must have been about three years old, he mused, old enough and wise enough to know that he would be kicked and punched if she found him before the rage wore off. His mother, a gorgeous, much-adored film star on the public stage and a drug-addled monster behind closed doors. That was the woman whose tender mercies his father had left him to rely on as a defenceless child.

And then, when he was twenty-six years old, everything had suddenly and quite miraculously changed. His half-brother, Argo, had died in a bungled mugging in a city street and without the smallest warning Heracles Antonakos had moved on surprisingly fast from his grief and had begun to take a passionate interest in the younger son he had snubbed for years. Of course, Jax's mother had been gone by then, Jax reminded himself ruefully, but he still could not adequately explain or understand the very abruptness of his father's change in attitude. Even so, the paternal recognition and support he had craved from his earliest years had unexpectedly and finally become his. Naturally he still wondered if his father's change of heart would last and life being what it was, of course, he had discovered a whole new set of challenges because life as the Antonakos heir was not all peaches and cream.

As the only son of one of the richest men in the world Jax had more money than he knew what to do with. Everywhere he went in Europe he was photographed and treated like a celebrity. Bands of adoring, manipulative and rapacious women tracked and hunted him much as if he were big game. But in the business field, he reminded himself with determined positivity, he had countless stimulating projects to command his interest and engage his brilliant mind.

One of Jax's bodyguards brought a phone to him, his expression dour and apologetic. Jax compressed his lips and accepted the predictable call from his father. Heracles ranted and raved in a rage about the risk Jax had taken by going on the race track and driving at breakneck speeds. Jax said nothing because over the past two years he had learned that arguing or trying to soothe only extended such frenzied sermons. Since Argo's shocking death, Heracles had developed a morbid and excessive fear of Jax participating in any activity that could possibly harm him and if he could have got away with wrapping his only surviving son in cotton wool and packing him away safely in a box he would have done so. While Jax valued his father's new apparent attachment to him even if he didn't quite trust it, he loathed the restrictive and interfering trappings of expectation that came with it.

Only for the sake of peace had Jax accepted the five heavily armed bodyguards he didn't need and who accompanied him everywhere he went. But he remained every bit as stubborn and fiercely independent as he had always been and when he felt the need to relieve stress he still went deep-sea diving, mountain climbing and flying. He still slept with unsuitable women as well…the sort of women even his father couldn't expect him to marry.

And why not? He loved being single and free as the air because he hated anyone trying to tell him what to do. On the only occasions he had strayed from that practical stance he had ended up in disastrous relationships, so now he didn't *ever* do relationships, he only did sex and uncomplicated sex at that. Once he had run off with another man's fiancée and barely lived to tell the tale, he recalled darkly.

Franca had crept into his bed one night when he was drunk and the deed of betrayal had been done before he'd even recognised *who* he was doing it with. Franca, of course, had simply used him to escape a life that had no longer suited her but he hadn't grasped that little fact. He had fallen hook, line and sinker for her 'damsel in distress' vibe long before he'd appreciated that he was dealing with a highly manipulative and destructive alcoholic. He had betrayed his friendship with his former business partner, Rio, but in the end he had more than paid his dues sorting Franca out. But had he learned? Had he hell. After Franca had come his second biggest mistake...

Yet another female-shaped mistake. So, he didn't want a wife and he didn't want children either and *nothing*, certainly not any dormant desire to please his long-absent father, was going to change that, he reflected cynically as Kat Valtinos approached him bearing drinks and a winning smile...

'I hate you doing work like this,' Kreon Thiarkis hissed under his breath as his daughter brought him a drink. 'It's demeaning—'

'Hard work is never demeaning, Dad,' Lucy declared, her dimples flashing as she smiled down soothingly at him. 'Don't be a snob. I'm not half as posh as you are and I never will be.'

Kreon bit back tart words of disagreement because he didn't want to hurt his daughter's feelings, most particularly because she had only been in his life for the last six months and he was afraid of driving her away by acting like a heavy-handed parent. After all, Lucy had never had a proper parent to look out for her, he acknowledged guiltily. But fiercely independent and proud as she was at twenty-one years old, she had been very much down on her luck when she'd finally approached Kreon, toting his baby granddaughter in her arms, both of them shabbily dressed and half starved. The older man's heart softened at the thought of little Bella, who was the most adorable toddler and the light of his life and his wife, Iola's, for he and Iola had met and married too late in life to have a family. He loved having the two of them in his home but he was firmly convinced that his daughter and her child still very much needed a husband to look after them when he himself was no longer around.

And that would have been *so* easy to achieve if only Lucy weren't so defensive and insecure, Kreon reflected in frustration, because his daughter was an extraordinarily beautiful girl. In the bar where she worked men stopped in their tracks simply to stare at her. With a mane of strawberry-blonde curls reaching halfway down her back, creamy skin and big blue eyes, she was a classic beauty and dainty as a doll. She made more on tips than any other waitress in the hotel and was, he had been reliably assured by the owner, who was a friend, a terrific asset to business.

Lucy went about her work, ruefully aware that the job she had insisted on taking only annoyed her father. Unfortunately, being a single parent was an expensive challenge even with the wonderful support her father and stepmother had given her in recent months. She was very grateful that she had come to Greece to finally meet her long-lost father for he and his wife had freely given both her and her daughter love, kindness and acceptance. Her father was the son of a Greek who had married an Englishwoman and he had grown up in London. Kreon was a wonderfully supportive parent and grandparent. Without a word of protest or reproach he had taken in Lucy and her child even though she hadn't warned him about Bella when he'd first invited her out to Greece.

But while Lucy was willing to accept free accommodation as well as her stepmother Iola's help as a sitter with Bella, she was determined not to become a permanent burden or to take too much advantage of the older couple's generosity. She was willing to admit that she had desperately needed help when she'd first arrived in Athens but she was trying very hard now to stand on her own two feet. Her earnings might be small but that salary meant she could pay for the necessities like clothing for herself and her child and for the moment that was enough to ease her pride.

As she stepped away from a customer, her boss and the hotel owner, Andreus, signalled to her. 'We're hosting an important business meeting here in the rear conference room tomorrow morning at eleven,' he informed her. 'I'd like you to serve the drinks and snacks. I only need you for a couple of hours but I'll pay you for a full shift.'

'I'll check with Iola but that should be fine because she doesn't usually go out in the morning,'

Lucy said, before taking off to serve a customer waving his hand in the air to get her attention.

The customer tried to chat her up and get her phone number but Lucy simply smiled politely and ignored his efforts because she wasn't even slightly interested in dating, or indeed in anything more physical, being well aware that the very fact she already had a child encouraged most men to assume that she would be a good bet for a casual encounter. She had been there, done that, lost the tee shirt and got a baby for her pains. Unhappily, as a green-as-grass nineteen-year-old virgin she hadn't grasped that she was involved in a casual fling until it was far too late to protect herself and she had been ditched. In fact, having been treated with such devastating contempt and dismissal by Bella's father, that final humiliation was still etched into her soul like a burn of shame that refused to heal whenever she thought about it…which was why she didn't allow herself to think about it *or* him very often.

In any case, what was the point in agonising over past mistakes and misjudgements, not to mention the most painful and cruel rejections she had suffered? Agonising never did change anything. Lucy had learned that the hard way time and time again when she was a vulnerable child growing up in care, subject to the whims of others and unable to control where she lived or even *who* she lived with. Now it meant that she found it hard to trust people and if she didn't have a certain amount of independence and choice she tended to feel horribly trapped and powerless.

But life, she reminded herself with dogged positivity, *was* getting better because for the first time in years she was daring to start putting down roots. She was happier than she had been in years and hoping to come up with a plan to improve her career prospects for Bella's sake. Very probably she would accept her father's offer to pay for some sort of job training or further education that would enable her to move out of low-paid employment. Perhaps it was finally time to start making some long-term decisions and think like a responsible adult, she told herself firmly.

'You're worth so much more than this kind of grunt work...' Bella's father had told Lucy two years earlier in Spain.

Well, look just how badly daring to have dreams and believe in them had turned out for her then, Lucy reflected, rigid with regret and pain as she stood at the bar to collect an order. Her friend at the time, another waitress called Tara, had been far more realistic about that relationship.

'He'll sleep with you and dump you and move on the minute he gets bored,' Tara had forecast, although the words she had used had been much earthier. 'Guys like that don't stick with girls like us. We're only good enough to party with for a few nights.'

Perspiration broke on Lucy's short upper lip and she wanted to punch herself hard for letting herself drift even momentarily down that bad memory lane, because hindsight only made her more ashamed of how stupid and naïve she had been. It was not as if she hadn't known what men were like, not as if she had grown up in some little princess castle, always protected and loved. She should have known better and she had yet to forgive herself for her rashness.

But at the end of her shift, when she got home to her father's very comfortable small town house and crept into the bedroom she shared with her daughter, she realised that nothing was quite that cut and dried. Bella slept nestled in her cot, curly black hair dark against the bedding, her olive skin flushed by sleep, long lashes screening her bright green eyes. Bella was gorgeous, like a little angel, Lucy thought with her eyes stinging and, although she could be sorry for everything else, she could not find it in her heart to regret Bella's existence in *any* way.

'Come with us to this dinner on Saturday night,' Iola urged over breakfast the next morning. She was a curvy brunette in her late forties with smiling dark eyes. 'It would please your father so much.'

Lucy went pink as she washed her daughter's face clean of breakfast debris. She knew that her dining out with them would please Kreon, but she also knew it would entail fending off the advances of at least two handpicked young men because her father's current main aim in life seemed to centre on finding her an eligible boyfriend. In that line Kreon was old-fashioned because he refused to credit that Lucy choosing to remain a single parent could be a viable plan for the future.

'Mum... Mum,' Bella carolled cheerfully as she was released from the high chair and set down to toddle somewhat clumsily round the room.

Lucy steadied her daughter as she almost fell over the toy box and ruffled her untidy curls. Curls, aside of the colour, just like her own, frizzy and ungovernable in humid weather, explosive when washed. Lucy looked back at her stepmother uncomfortably. She felt like an ungrateful brat for her reluctance to do what her father wanted her to do. 'I'm just not interested in meeting anyone at present...maybe in a few months I'll feel differently,' she added without much conviction.

'You had a bad breakup and you went through a lot alone afterwards,' Iola acknowledged gently. 'But your father's a man and he doesn't get it. I did try to explain to him that this is more of a healing time for you—'

'Yes, that's it, that's *exactly* it!' Lucy exclaimed, giving the older woman a sudden impulsive and appreciative hug. 'I'm not ready right now, not sure if I'll ever be though...'

'Not all men are like Bella's father. There *are* decent caring men out there,' Iola reminded her quietly.

'Nobody knows that better than me. I kissed a lot of frogs before I met Kreon.'

Lucy grinned and then laughed because her stepmother really did understand her viewpoint. A few minutes later, she left the town house and set out to walk to the small select Hotel Palati where she worked. Sited in an exclusive district in Athens, the hotel catered mainly to a business clientele.

Her father had met Iola when he'd engaged her as a PA in a property rental business that had eventually gone bust. But then Kreon had led a chequered 'boom to bust and back again' life and had been divorced once for infidelity. Lucy had respected his honesty with her. Even on the subject of her late mother, Kreon had proved to be painfully frank. Kreon hadn't once whitewashed his own failings or hidden the fact that he had gained a criminal record over some pyramid selling scheme he had got involved with as a younger man. Yet in spite of that honesty, Lucy still wasn't quite sure what actually funded her father's comfortable lifestyle.

She knew that Kreon gambled and took bets on a near professional basis and that he was always enthusiastically involved in some hopefully lucrative business scheme of one kind or another. Whatever he did, he seemed to be successful at it. Even so, she would not have been entirely surprised to learn that some of his ventures skated a little too close to the edge of breaking the law. But basically because he and Iola had given Lucy and her daughter both the home and the love Lucy had never known before, she closed her eyes to that suspicion and minded her own business the best she could.

After all, there truly *were* shades of grey between the black and white of absolute right and absolute wrong, she ruminated ruefully. Nothing and nobody was perfect. Even at the height of her passionate infatuation with Jax, she had recognised that he was flawed and all too human. He had been moody, controlling, domineering and arrogant and they had fought like cat and dog on a regular basis because, while Lucy might be only five feet tall and undersized, she was no pushover. At heart, she was stubborn and gutsy and quick-tempered. Even if Jax hadn't let her down so horribly, it would never have worked between them, she reasoned, feeling pleasantly philosophical on that score and firmly stifling the painful little push of heartache that still hollowed out her tummy. So, she'd had her heart broken just as Iola and thousands of other women *and* men had. It had only made her more resilient and less foolish and naïve, she told herself squarely.

The hotel manager showed her into the lofty-ceilinged back room, which had been comprehensively redecorated only weeks earlier with an opulence that was calculated to appeal to the more discerning customers.

Sometimes when Lucy daydreamed she wondered, if she had come from a more fortunate background, would she have become one of the elegant well-educated young businesswomen she saw round the hotel. Unfortunately she had been handicapped at the outset of life by her birth. Her parents' marriage had broken down after her mother had had an affair.

'Annabel always thought some better man was waiting for her round the next corner,' Kreon had said wryly of Lucy's mother. 'I wasn't rich and I lived by my wits and she had big ideas. We were living in London then where she was struggling to get the finance to set up her nursery business. But my father had returned to Greece after my mother died and he fell ill out here. I *had* to go to him. When I left London I had no idea Annabel was pregnant and when I contacted her to tell her that I was coming back she told me we were finished because she had met someone else. Now from what you're telling me, it seems she may have learned that she had this dreadful disease and she didn't want me around even though she had my child. I can't understand that, I will *never* understand that...'

And Lucy couldn't understand it either because, just listening to Kreon talking, she had recognised that he *had* loved her mother and had planned to return to London to be with her. But the more Kreon had spoken of her mother's beauty and her feverish love and need for fresh male attention, the more Lucy had suspected that there definitely *had* been

another man and Annabel had burnt her boats for
ever with Kreon shortly before illness had cruelly
claimed her future.

Lucy had been two years old when Annabel was
hospitalised and her daughter put into care. Her only
memory of her mother was of a beautiful redhead
lying in bed and shouting at her, so she wasn't sure
that the mother who had surrendered her to the authorities had been that much of a loss in the parent
stakes. Kreon had described a flighty, selfish personality, ill-suited to the kind of personal sacrifices
a mother was often forced to make. And when, to
Lucy's very great astonishment, Kreon had revealed
that Annabel had actually had two other daughters
being raised by her own mother somewhere in northern England, Lucy had been silenced by that shat-
tering news.

Apparently she had two half-sisters somewhere,
born from her mother's previous liaisons. Some day
Lucy planned to look into that startling discovery
but she didn't even know where you started in such a
search because, not only had she no money to pursue
enquiries, but also no names even to begin with. Naturally all these years on Kreon didn't recall such details about Annabel's background and history. After
all, he had never met Annabel's mother and had been
stonewalled by Annabel when he'd asked to do so.
All he had remembered was that Annabel never went
to visit the two little girls she had left behind her and

he had said that even then he had recognised that as a warning sign that Annabel's attachments were of the shallow sort.

Lucy had counted herself lucky that she was not equally superficial because she adored Bella and would have laid down her life for her child, counting Bella as one of the few good developments in a life that had been far from easy or happy. On the other hand, had she cared less about Jax she would have been less devastated when he disappeared. My goodness, she had fallen apart at the seams and done stupid stuff, she recalled ruefully. She had been thrown off his father's yacht and warned never to show her face at the marina again while being marched off by security guards. She had been shouted at, called nasty names and utterly humiliated in her fruitless pursuit of Jax. All because she was fundamentally stupid, she conceded with regret.

After all, it had been crazy of her to believe that she meant anything more to Jax than an easily forgettable sexual fling, and when he was done with a woman, he was definitely *done*. The crewman on the yacht had called her a cheap whore as he'd bodily manhandled her off the polished deck and forced her down the gangway. She had fallen, been hurt and bruised by that brutality and she had been pregnant at the time. That was one reason she had never told her father the whole truth about Bella's parentage, preferring him to assume that Bella was the result of some one-night stand with a man in Spain. She knew Kreon would seek revenge and restitution if she ever told him the whole story.

So, in a way, staying silent was protecting her father from doing anything rash, she reasoned uneasily. Kreon was extremely protective. He would hit the roof if he realised that Lucy had been homeless even though Bella's father was a rich man, who could so easily have helped her and their child. A rich man, who was also Greek. That information wouldn't help either when Kreon was so immensely proud of his heritage.

But then Lucy had long since decided that rich people were pretty much untouchable, unlike the rest of humanity. The very rich had the power and the money to hold the rest of the world at bay and she saw the evidence of that galling fact every time she saw Jax in the media. Jax surrounded by bodyguards and beautiful women, never alone, never approachable, as protected and distanced from ordinary people as an exhibit in a locked museum case. Jax Antonakos, renowned entrepreneur and billionaire in his own right with a daddy who had billions also.

Her hands trembled as she set out china on the trolley awaiting her. She hated Jax now with the same passion she had once put into loving him. He had strung her along, faked so many things and she could never, ever forgive the fact that he had quite deliberately left her stranded in Spain without a home or a job or any means of support. That she had been pregnant into the bargain was just her bad luck, but then Lucy had little experience of good luck.

A cluster of chattering businessmen entered and she served the coffee, standing back by the wall to dutifully await any further requests. Beyond the ajar door there was a burst of comment and then a sudden hush and the sound of many footsteps crossing the tiled hallway outside. The door whipped back noisily on its hinges and two men strode in, talking into ear pieces while checking the exit doors and all the windows, and that level of security warned Lucy that someone tremendously important was evidently about to arrive. The security men backed against the wall in silence and two more arrived to take up stances on the other side of the room. The almost militaristic security detail seemed so over the top for a small business meeting that Lucy almost laughed out loud.

And then Jax walked in and she stopped breathing and any desire to laugh died in her suddenly constricted lungs...

CHAPTER TWO

THE INSTANT LUCY saw that untidy black hair and the gorgeous green eyes so arrestingly bright against his bronzed skin, she wanted to run and keep on running and only innate discipline kept her where she was while she questioned her reaction. Why should *she* want to run? What had she done to be ashamed of? She was not a coward, she had never been a coward, she reminded herself doggedly, unnerved by that craven desire to flee. Indeed if anyone should be embarrassed it should be Jax for the cruel way he had treated her.

Couples broke up all the time but the process didn't have to be downright nasty. She hadn't been a stalker. There had been no excuse for threats and no need whatsoever to run her out of the neighbourhood.

Recollecting that vicious goodbye, Lucy lifted her chin high. Seated centre stage at the circular table, the cynosure of all attention and conversation, Jax mercifully wasn't looking round the room enough to notice her. Lucy might have overcome the urge to run but it did annoy her to find herself in a subservient role in Jax's radius again. In a mad moment she had once fantasised about swanning through some swanky club some day looking like a million dollars and seeing Jax and totally ignoring him to demonstrate her disdain and overall superiority as a decent human being. But now that she was actually on the spot she discovered that she was indefensibly and horribly curious and could only stare at him.

He had kept his black hair short. Once he had worn it long but he had had it cropped not long after she'd first met him, hitting the more conventional note she had suspected his father preferred. In retrospect she found it hard to credit that they had once bonded over their absent fathers. Jax had admitted how recently his father had come back into his life and had shared his grief over the death of the half-brother he had loved, not to mention his mother's abuse and infidelities. None of those deep conversations had fitted into what she assumed could be described as a typical short-term fling. But then that was Jax, a tough individualist, unpredictable, fiery and mysterious…the archetypal brooding hero beloved of teenaged girls with an overly romantic disposition, she concluded sourly.

That he *was* startlingly handsome had undoubtedly influenced the fantasies she had woven, she acknowledged, chewing at her lower lip, fingernails biting painfully into her palms. High cheekbones, strong clean jaw line, stunning eyes set beneath well-shaped ebony brows. Of course his mother had been a very famous and stunningly beautiful Spanish movie star and he had inherited her looks. In a big magazine article she had once read about him, which had been accompanied by a close-up photo, the journalist had raved about those dazzling wild green eyes and the spiky length of his sooty lashes.

Bella had *his* eyes. Lucy swallowed hard, recalling her feelings as her daughter's blue eyes at birth had slowly transformed to an eerily familiar emerald in her innocent little face. Innocent, something Jax was not and had never been. And reading about his sexual exploits over the past two years had helped Lucy to understand that he had always been a selfish, ruthless womaniser but she had been too trusting and inexperienced to recognise his true nature. Her heart was fluttering a beat so fast behind her breastbone that she wanted to press a hand against it to slow it down.

And then the truth of her response hit her and she was aghast that in spite of everything her body could still react to the presence of his. He glanced up from the file he had been perusing and for a split second, a literal *single* heartbeat, she clashed in dismay with his fierce gaze. It was like an electric shock pulsing low in her pelvis, tightening bone and sinew, awakening sensations she had almost forgotten and had never felt since. Every pulse she possessed went crazy, her breath catching in her throat, her very skin as achingly sensitive as if he had actually *touched* her. And then that tiny moment was over and past as Jax blanked her and passed the file back to someone at the table while making some comment about profit margins.

Her Greek vocabulary was slowly growing but in unfamiliar scenarios she still got as lost as any non-Greek-speaking foreigner. And *of course* Jax was going to blank her, she told herself shakily. Had she really thought he would greet a worker bee as low on the proverbial food chain as a waitress? Her mouth compressed as she wondered anxiously how he would react to the news that he was a father were she to tell him. With furious hostility and denial, she reckoned, her skin turning clammy at the prospect. Jax had once been very upfront about the fact that he didn't ever want children. Bearing that in mind, Lucy ruminated grimly, he should have been more careful to ensure that he didn't get her pregnant.

Jax's lean, chiselled features were rigid. He refused to look back in Lucy's direction. He didn't need to. That momentary image was stamped into his brain like a punch. What the hell was she doing in Athens? And her sudden appearance in his presence? Some sort of a set-up? And if so, why? Jax never took anything at face value any more. After all, he had once accepted Lucy for what she appeared to be and learned his very great error.

Bile tinged his mouth as he briefly recalled what he had read in that investigation file on her background: a string of drug offences stretching back years and convictions for soliciting sex. He had felt like a complete idiot. He had rushed off to see her, *confront* her even though it was late at night and then he had seen who she really was for himself…down an alley with a man enthusiastically giving up what she had made him wait weeks to enjoy.

Disgust and distaste flooded Jax, bringing back even less welcome memories of his mother's rampant promiscuity and empty promises of fidelity. He had seen her cheating break more than one man who had adored her. His father didn't know it because he had never dared to ask what his son's life had been like with his mother but Heracles had not been the only man to be chewed up and spat out in pieces by Mariana, who had wilfully followed every stray sexual impulse. As for Lucy, she was a liar and a cheat and he did not forgive betrayal. The entire episode had been sordid in the extreme. So why was he remembering that she had given him the wildest, hottest sex he had ever had?

A stubborn push of raunchily sexual images infiltrated Jax's hind brain even while he fought to hold them at bay and kept on talking about the project on the table. Hard as a rock behind his zip, Jax went rigid with angry aggression. How dared Lucy even walk into a room that contained him? He had always told himself that he had not inherited his father's notorious temper and equally notorious ability to hold a grudge but just then he recognised that he had lied to himself. Had it been possible to bodily throw Lucy out, he would have done so!

One of the bodyguards nudged Lucy's elbow and she glanced up, dragged from her own bemused thoughts with a vengeance. The older man indicated the coffee on the trolley and angled his head in his employer's direction, clearly urging her to get on with her job.

Reddening all the way up to her hairline, Lucy unfroze in an effort to behave normally. Even so she had to fight a huge inner battle to force her legs over to the trolley and pour Jax a coffee when all she really wanted to do was empty the entire contents of the pot over his hateful, arrogant head. Without him looking once at her or indeed acknowledging her in any way, she settled the coffee at his elbow with a hand that trembled slightly. Next she laid out the snacks and topped up the cups, signalling the bar waiter at the door when one of the men requested a shot of ouzo to wash down his coffee.

From below screening lashes and the almost infinitesimal movements of his proud dark head, Jax tracked Lucy's every move like a predator planning an attack. A blinding flash of memory assailed him:

skin as translucent as fine porcelain in the dawn light, his fingers knotted into tumbling golden ringlets spread across a pillow, glorious bright blue eyes holding his, a tiny slender body with surprisingly sexy little curves reaching up to his. A little curvier than she used to be, he estimated abstractedly, remembering for a few seconds and then suddenly emerging again from that uncharacteristic reverie to answer a question, angrier and hotter than he had been in years.

The louse could at least have thanked her for the coffee, Lucy reflected with growing annoyance. Even a nod would have been acceptable but then Jax had always been a law unto himself, ferociously uncompromising and challenging, driven to succeed, survive and flourish as if it was in his genes. And perhaps it was. Only in a fantasy could there ever have been a scenario in which she believed that Jax Antonakos would settle down with a humble waitress... Bitterness gripped her and resentment shot through her like a sheet of lightning flashing off all her exposed nerve endings with painful effect.

Who the hell did Jax Antonakos think he was to treat her with such derisive dismissal?

Jax summoned Zenas, his head security guard, with an almost imperceptible flicker of his gaze and passed him a note. Zenas stood back to read it and confusion gripped his features for an instant before discipline kicked in and he left the room to do his employer's bidding. Lucy paid little heed to the by-play and only tensed when her own boss appeared in the doorway and silently summoned her out into the hallway.

A frown line bisected the older man's brow as he studied her. 'Mr Antonakos wants to speak to you in private when he's finished. I'm not sure how your father would feel about that request—'

Comprehension gripped Lucy fast. Andreus had no idea that she already knew Jax. He simply thought that Jax was trying to get off with her.

'Please don't mention this to Dad,' she muttered unevenly, for that was not a connection she wanted made. Once a link of any kind was established, secrets could spill out.

Andreus cast open the door of a smaller room across the corridor. 'Wait in there…but only if you *want* to,' he added with deliberate meaning. 'This is nothing to do with your employment here or with me. I have only passed on his request because I am very reluctant to offend so powerful a man.'

Lucy turned a slow, painful red, rage mushrooming inside her again as she imagined what her employer must be thinking. Jax wouldn't care about appearances. Jax had never *had* to care about appearances. For an instant she almost walked away from the opportunity to tell Jax what she thought of him. But she was too nervous, too aware of what had happened the last time her very existence nearby had become objectionable to Jax Antonakos. He had paid her then boss in Spain to sack her and she had lost her job and the accommodation that went with it. That was the kind of power the super wealthy had. Her boss in those days had been outrageously frank with her, admitting that he couldn't afford to keep her on when so much money to do otherwise was on offer and that he had had a poor summer season.

She paced the floor in the small room that was normally used as an office by the hotel housekeeper, thinking herself lucky that Jax hadn't had a room in the hotel and called her there, which would have looked even worse. Why on earth after ignoring her would he have demanded a meeting? From his point of view that made no sense, she reasoned with a frown. After all, he had ditched her two years earlier without an explanation or even a text. He hadn't turned up for their last date, hadn't phoned, hadn't done anything and when she had tried to contact him he had blocked her calls. Either he had simply tired of her or she had done or said something that had offended.

It hurt to look back and recall how many weeks she had tormented herself by pathetically wondering what she had done to annoy Jax. But nothing could have justified his subsequent behaviour in having her sacked and forced to leave the area like some vagrant whose very presence was offensive. That more than anything was what she could not forgive.

'You literally have three minutes or you'll miss your flight,' Zenas warned Jax outside the door.

Jax strode into the room, absently wondering if there was actual truth in the idea that human beings needed closure following certain experiences because he could not imagine any other reason why he should still feel driven to confront Lucy. Two years ago, he had never wanted to see or speak to her again. But possibly curiosity provided more motivation than he was willing to admit, he reasoned impatiently, angry tension tightening his lean, darkly handsome features.

'What the hell are you doing in Athens?' Jax demanded.

Lucy spun round from the window to face him, inwardly reeling from the shock of Jax in the flesh standing close enough to touch. He was so tall and he radiated restive energy and dominant vibes in waves. Tensing, she lifted her head up but she still had to tip it back to actually see any part of him above chest level. Not for the first time her diminutive height struck her as an embarrassing flaw. Being almost child-sized often meant that people didn't take her seriously or treat her like an adult. 'What's that got to do with you?' she slung back sharply, her tone similar to his own.

Jax drew himself up to his full six-foot-three-inch height and glowered down at her, green eyes luminescent with rage because it had been two years since anyone but his father had challenged him. 'Answer me,' he ground out impatiently.

'I don't owe you any answers... I don't owe you the time of day,' Lucy traded with the kind of provocation that struck a deep and unwelcome note of familiarity with Jax.

'You *will* answer me,' Jax raked back at her in a raw undertone, watching as she angled her head back and struck an attitude, hand on hip. Strawberry golden curls slid round her shoulders, her hair falling round her heart-shaped face, accentuating the defiant blue of her eyes and the lush fullness of her rosy lips.

And that fast, that urgently, Jax wanted to throw her down on the desk and control her the only way he had ever really controlled her, with the seething passion that was the mainstay of his character. For the briefest of moments he allowed himself to imagine the hot, wet tightness of her and the pulse at his groin reacted with unbridled enthusiasm. He reminded himself that it had been a toxic relationship and that she had played him like a con artist with her stories, her fake innocence and her lies. A dizzy surge of rage ignited inside him like a threatening fireball.

'If you don't answer me you will live to regret it,' Jax threatened in a wrathful undertone, every drop of his merciless Antonakos blood burning through him and hungry for a fight.

An angry spurt of fear made Lucy's stomach turn

over sickly. He was too influential to challenge as even her boss had reminded her. She knew Jax could cause trouble for her, maybe even for her father as well if she wasn't careful. She might hate Jax but it would be insane to risk such penalties. 'What am I doing in Athens?' she repeated flatly. 'I finally looked up my birth father and he lives here—'

'But that was all lies,' Jax breathed in momentary bewilderment. 'You don't *have* a Greek father.'

Her smooth brow furrowed with genuine confusion. 'Lies? I don't know what you're talking about. I believe my birth certificate is as accurate as anyone else's. At the moment I'm living with my father and his wife.'

'That's not possible,' Jax told her, stiffening as a light knock on the door warned him that their time was up if he planned to make it to the airport. His long, lean frame swivelled as he half turned towards the door to leave, common sense and practicality powering him.

'I just want you to know that I hate you and I'll never forgive you for what you did to me,' Lucy confided in a belated rush of angry frustration that she could not tell him what she really thought of him any more bluntly than that. In truth she wanted to scream at him, she wanted to throw herself at him and hammer him with angry fists for hurting her.

'I didn't *do* anything to you,' Jax parried with complete cool.

'It was vicious...what you did, unnecessary!' Lucy condemned chokily, bitterness almost overpowering her along with a very human need to hit back. 'Having me sacked? Leaving me penniless and homeless and forced to go back to the UK when I had nothing there!'

An ebony brow elevated at that improbable accusation of bullying behaviour on his part, Jax swung back to her just as another knock sounded on the door. Whatever else he might be, Jax prided himself on never having treated a woman badly. 'I don't have time for this and I shouldn't make time for it either,' he acknowledged grimly. 'You're a liar and a cheat—'

'Of course you're going to say stuff like that, rewrite history, because you're so up yourself now,' Lucy shot back at him in disgust as she thought about her innocent, trusting little daughter. 'But I never lied to you or cheated on you and you never once thought about consequences, did you?'

He wanted her phone number but he wouldn't ask for it, wouldn't allow himself to ask for it. He knew what she was. He didn't want anything to do with her. So, having reached that decision and feeling invigorated by it, he could not explain why he then turned back like a man with a split personality and told her to meet him for a drink the following evening at a little bar he patronised on the marina, a haunt of his for quiet moments, which the paparazzi had yet to discover. Even as he walked back out again, he was questioning the decision and regretting it, lean brown hands clenching into impatient fists. What the hell had he done that for?

But what had she meant by 'consequences'? And how come she *did* have a Greek father when according to that file she did not?

He was simply curious, nothing wrong or surprising about that. His libido was not in the driver's seat, he assured himself with solid conviction. Stray memories had briefly aroused him when he saw her again, nothing more meaningful. All men remembered incredibly good sex. Furthermore, he had a little black book of phonebook proportions to turn to when he felt like sex, hot and cold running women on tap wherever he travelled. *That* was the world he lived in. There was no way he could ever be tempted to revisit a manipulative little cheat like Lucy Dixon, he reflected with satisfaction.

Naturally, becoming the Antonakos heir had ensured that Jax became significantly more cynical about women. He didn't listen to sob stories any more, he didn't let his inherently dangerous streak of chivalry rule him. Indeed the sight of a woman in need of rescue was more like aversion therapy to him now. He knew from experience that that kind of woman was likely to be far more trouble than she was worth.

After all, how many times had he felt he had no

choice but to race to his mother's rescue? When the men she betrayed became violent as her lies were exposed? When she needed another spell in some discreet rehabilitation facility before she could be seen in public again? When he was forced to lie to protect *her*?

And yet at heart he had always known that his mother was a deeply disturbed and egocentric human being, undeserving of his care and respect. That was why his little sister, Tina, had died, he reminded himself bitterly. Mariana's self-centred neglect of her younger child had directly led to the incident in which the toddler had drowned. But he had only been fourteen, so what could he possibly have done when so many adults had witnessed the insanity of his mother's lifestyle and yet failed to act to protect either of her children?

Lucy walked home in a pensive mood. Of course she wouldn't meet him, she told herself firmly. What would be the point? *Bella!* Jax was a father whether he liked it or not but she knew he wouldn't like that news any more than he liked her. And why was her being in Greece such a big deal? What was it to him? It was not as though they were likely to bump into each other again in normal life. Jax lived against a backdrop of massive yachts, private jets and private islands. He didn't rub shoulders with ordinary working people.

Yet a giant ball of despair was threatening to swal-

low Lucy up and she didn't know why. Seeing Jax
again, she recognised, had *hurt* and hurt much more
than she had expected. It had brought back memories she didn't want. She had loved him and had
given her trust to a man for the first time ever. His
sudden volte-face had almost destroyed her because
she had given him so much she had felt bare to the
world without him.

And yet he *still* wasn't married. She had thought
for sure that he would marry the wealthy heiress his
father kept pushing in his direction, the very lovely
but very bitchy Kat Valtinos. But then Jax was bone-
deep stubborn. You could take a horse to water but
you couldn't make it drink and getting Jax to do anything he didn't want to do was like trying to push a
boulder up a steep hill.

Kat Valtinos had organised the party the night
Lucy had met Jax on his father's enormous yacht.
Lucy's memory wafted her back two years into the
past. Back then, Jax had been in Spain setting up
a new resort on the coast. When the caterers had
mucked up with a double booking, Kat had person-
ally trawled through the local bars seeking waitresses
for the event.

'You two will do,' she had said to Lucy and Tara,
looking them up and down as though they were au-
ditioning as strippers. 'You're young and pretty and
sexy. Just what men like. You put your make-up on
with a trowel,' she had told Tara critically and to

Lucy she had said, 'You need to show more leg and cleavage.'

If the money hadn't been so good, Lucy wouldn't have done it but back then she had lived on a budget where no tips meant stale bread and going hungry. Their boss didn't feed them for free and they had no cooking facilities in their mean little attic room, which had been hot as hell up under the eaves above the restaurant kitchen. Any extra cash was deeply welcome in those days.

The party had been full of blowhard bellicose men talking themselves up in Antonakos's company and drinking too much. One of them had cornered Lucy when she was sent to a lower deck to restock the bar from the supplies stored there. She had been trying to fight him off when Jax had intervened. Jax, blue-black glossy hair brushing his shoulders, green eyes glittering like shards of glass, who had dragged the guy off her with punishing hands and hit him hard without hesitation.

'Are you OK?' the most gorgeous guy she had ever seen had asked, pulling her off the wall she had slumped against, smoothing down the skirt the creep had been trying to wrench up. '*Diavolos*, you're so tiny. Did he hurt you?'

'Only a little,' she had said shakily, trembling like a leaf and in absolutely no doubt that Jax had saved her from a serious assault because, with the noisy party taking place on the deck above, the lower deck had been deserted and nobody would have heard her crying out.

'Take a moment to recover,' Jax had urged, guiding her into an opulent saloon to push her down into a seat where her cotton-wool legs had collapsed under her as if he had flipped a switch. 'What were you doing down here on this deck?'

He had issued instructions on the phone to a crew member to have the bar supplies refreshed. And the whole time she had just been staring at him like a brainless idiot, utterly intimidated by everything about him from the expensive quality of his lightweight grey suit and hand-stitched shoes to the sheer beauty of his perfect features from his edgy cheekbones to his sculpted mouth. It was the eyes that had got to her the most, the tender concern she'd seen there and then the budding all-male appreciation. He had the most stunning eyes and his rare smile had been like the sun coming out on a dark day.

'Are you OK?' he repeated.

Well, no, in fact from that moment she had never been OK again. Something she'd needed to survive had lurched into strange territory and softened to let him in, no matter that it had gone against sense and practicality and her life experience. She had truly never been the same since.

CHAPTER THREE

LUCY WAS RIVEN with extreme guilt by the time she finally climbed on the bus that would take her down to the marina.

She had had to lie to Iola simply to get out. She had pretended that she was joining a couple of the other waitresses for a few drinks. To weigh down her conscience even more, Iola had been delighted to believe that her stepdaughter was finally going out and about. Her stepmother had hovered helpfully, urging her to put on make-up and wear the pretty white sundress that Iola had bought for her a few weeks earlier. But how *could* Lucy have admitted that she was heading out to meet Bella's father? After all, she had already lied on that subject by declaring that she had no way of getting in touch with the man who had fathered her daughter. Kreon and Iola had averted their eyes in dismay and embarrassment at that claim, clearly assuming that she did not know the man's name.

Indeed, one lie only led to more lies, Lucy conceded shamefacedly, annoyed that she had found it impossible to be more honest. But Kreon would raise the roof if he discovered that Jax was Bella's father and she didn't want to put Kreon in the potential firing line of Antonakos displeasure.

And why was she off to meet Jax when she had sworn she would not do so?

Obviously she was thinking about her daughter's needs, wondering if there was any chance that Jax could have changed his outlook on children and could possibly be willing to embrace the news that he was a parent. It was definitely her duty to check out that possibility and finally tell him that he had a child, she told herself staunchly even while her heart hammered and her breath caught in her throat at the prospect of seeing Jax again.

You're pathetic, she scolded herself angrily as she marched past crowded bars, ignoring the men who called out to her. He's a very good-looking guy and of course you still notice that but that's all, leave it there. You are *not* a silly impulsive teenager any more, she coached herself, you know what he is and what he's like and *you know better*.

Jax lounged outside the bar with Zenas close by, the rest of his security detail settled within hailing distance. He didn't know why he had come until he saw Lucy, her dress flowing and dancing round her slender knees, the pristine white lighting up below the street lights, her strawberry-blonde ringlets a vivid fall round her narrow shoulders. And then he knew why he had come and he hated that surge of absolute primal lust, raw distaste flaming through him even as his jeans became uncomfortably tight. A wave of male heads slowly turned to check her out as she passed by. Jax gritted his even white teeth at that familiar display.

'The waitress…*really*?' Zenas teased from the shadows.

'I need to have this conversation in private,' Jax warned his old school friend quietly, relieved that Zenas had only joined the team the year before and had no idea of his prior acquaintance with Lucy.

Zenas strolled obediently across the street and plonked himself down on a bench. Jax lifted his newspaper, refusing to continue watching Lucy walk towards him, perturbed by the level of his own interest. He would get answers from her, satisfy his curiosity and leave. There would be nothing more personal and absolutely *no* sex.

Lucy saw Jax outside the bar, arrogant dark head bent, the bold cut of his chiselled profile golden beneath the lights, his black hair still long enough to tousle in the light breeze. And her heart bounced inside her like a rubber ball because she was helplessly reliving the excitement he had always induced in her. There were flutters in her tummy, crazy tingles pinching the tips of her breasts taut and a dangerous hot, liquid awareness pulsing into being between her legs. Just as quickly her entire body felt overheated and she was seriously embarrassed for herself.

As she took a seat Jax glanced up at her from below his ridiculously long lashes, crescents of uncompromising green running assessingly across her flushed face. 'At least you're on time for once... I assume you hurried.'

Lucy blinked and bit down on her tongue hard. Her poor timekeeping had always infuriated Jax because he hated being kept waiting and never, ever understood how time could sometimes run away from her. He had always contended that being late was rude and indefensible. But then Jax, who was relentlessly practical and full of ferocious initiative in tough scenarios, had probably never had a weakness for daydreaming.

Daydreaming, however, had always been Lucy's escape from challenging experiences. When she didn't fit in at the many different schools she had attended she had floated away on a fluffy cloud inside her own mind. When life was especially difficult, fantasies had become her consolation and she would dream of a world in which she had love and security and happiness.

In the smouldering silence that had now fallen, Lucy forced herself out of her abstraction and registered that Jax was watching her with impatient green eyes as if he had guessed that she had momentarily drifted away with the fairies. In receipt of that aggravated look, she felt her mouth run dry as a bone. In desperation she spun his newspaper round, her attention falling on a recent custody case that had attracted a lot of media coverage. 'Oh, my goodness…' she muttered as she slowly traced the headline with a fingertip while she carefully translated it. 'The *father* got the kid? How could they take a child away from his mother?'

Jax shrugged an uninterested shoulder as he signalled the waiter. 'Why not? Life has moved on. Fathers are now equal to mothers—'

'Yes, but—'

'Read it and you'll see why the family court reached that decision,' Jax said drily.

'I can't read Greek well enough yet,' she admitted grudgingly.

'The father is willing to work at home to be with the child while the mother would be leaving him in a nursery all day. Why are we talking about this anyway?' Jax demanded impatiently.

'It's an interesting case,' Lucy proffered stiffly. 'The mother's a paramedic who doesn't have the option of working at home.'

'While the father wants his child and what's best for his child, which is as it should be,' Jax interposed as a bottle of wine and glasses arrived at the table.

A cold skitter of fear pierced Lucy's tense body as a glass of wine appeared in front of her. 'Is that how you would feel?'

'We're not talking about me. I won't be fathering any children,' Jax declared with a cynical twist of his expressive mouth. 'Don't need the hassle or the responsibility. But if I *did* have a child I certainly wouldn't sit back and allow a woman to take my child away from me…in fact that is the very last thing I would do.'

A quiver of sheer fright rippled down Lucy's taut spine as she reached for her wine. That risk, that particular fear of losing her child, had never once crossed her mind as a possibility. And why hadn't it? Jax might not want children but he *was* a very possessive guy. What was his was very much his, not to be shared or touched or even looked at by anyone else. Once he had treated Lucy like that, enraging her with his determination to own her body and soul and control her every move. Suppose she told him about Bella and he felt the same way about his daughter?

Sobered by that fear, Lucy decided there and then to continue keeping Bella a secret until she had, at least, taken legal advice. In fact maybe the legal route would be the best way to go when it came to breaking that news, she thought cravenly. It would be more impersonal and less likely to lead to confrontation and bad feeling. Just at that moment Lucy could not face telling Jax that he was the father of her child and that because of his behaviour after their breakup she had had no way of telling him that she was pregnant. That was not her fault, she reminded herself. That was unquestionably *his* fault.

'When did you move to Athens?' Jax prompted.

'Six months ago... I was struggling to make ends meet in London,' she confided, almost rolling her eyes at that severe understatement before taking several fortifying swallows of wine.

'When we talked in Spain, you had no plans to track your father down,' he reminded her with a frown. 'You thought he had deserted your mother and you *said*—'

'I was wrong. When I needed help, my father came through for me,' Lucy admitted. 'Why did you ask me to meet you?'

Jax watched her sip at the wine, one little finger rubbing back and forth over the stem of the glass, her lush mouth rosy and moist. Like a sex-starved adolescent, he remembered the feel of her mouth, the flick of her teasing little tongue and he went rigid.

'*Jax?*' she pressed, setting down the glass.

Lean, dark features taut, Jax topped up the wine. He had tried to teach her about wine once: how to select it, savour it, how to truly *taste* it, and she was still knocking it back as if it were cheap plonk. That had been another lesson that had inexplicably ended up between the sheets. But then nothing had ever gone to plan with Lucy. His self-discipline had vanished. When he had taken her shopping he had taken

her in the changing cubicle up against the wall, stifling her frantic cries with his hand. Yes, she had
definitely *earned* that red dress he had later seen her
wearing while she gave her body to another man.

'Why?' Lucy prompted in growing frustration at
his brooding silence.

Jax inclined his head to Zenas and spoke to him
soft and low when he approached. 'We'll go somewhere more private—'

Lucy collided with smouldering green eyes like
highly polished emeralds and stiffened in instant rejection of that idea. 'No.'

'I don't know what I was thinking of. This is not
the place to talk.' Or fight, Jax reflected, in no doubt
that angry words were likely to be exchanged when
he challenged her.

Lucy gulped down more wine in an effort to
steady herself and think carefully before she spoke.
'I don't want to go anywhere else with you,' she argued.

'Don't lie,' Jax advised in the driest of tones. 'I
could have you on your back in five minutes if that's
what I wanted…but it's *not*.'

A tide of outraged colour slowly dappled Lucy's
creamy skin as she gazed back at him, aghast at his
crudity. 'I can't believe you said that.'

Jax shrugged again, a knowing look in his stunning eyes. 'It's only what we're both thinking about.'

Lucy bristled like a cat stroked the wrong way

and threw her shoulders back. 'No, it's not. Speak for yourself.'

'I fell for the virgin ploy once. Don't push your luck, *koukla mou*,' Jax advised as he thrust back his chair and began to rise. 'Born-again virgins push the wrong buttons with me.'

'Don't call me that... I'm *not* anyone's doll!' Lucy protested, aware of the meaning of those words because her father used them around Bella.

'Don't push your luck, Tinker Bell,' Jax stabbed instead.

And the sound of that once familiar pet name hurt like the unexpected swipe of a knife across tender skin. It turned her pale because it took her back to a place she didn't want to go, to a period when she had fondly believed herself to be loved and safe and cherished. But it had all been a lie and a seriously cruel lie at that. It hurt even more that she had adored that lie and longed for it to last for ever and ever, just like in the fairy tales.

'You still haven't told me what this is about,' Lucy argued as she drank down her wine with desperate little swallows that pained her throat. 'I'm staying here.'

A long silver limousine purred along the kerb. They were in a pedestrian zone and the car shouldn't have been there but the two police officers lounging across the street did nothing to interfere with its progress.

'Get in the car or I'll throw you in it!' Jax bit out in a driven undertone, what little patience he had taxed by her obstinacy.

He had made a mistake, he thought furiously, turning his head and unexpectedly encountering Zenas's shocked appraisal, registering that the other man had heard that threat.

Incredulous, Lucy giggled. 'You wouldn't dare,' she told him.

And he *did*. He picked her up off the chair and shoved her into the back seat of the limo as if she were a lost parcel he was retrieving, aware throughout that his bodyguards were watching him as if he had gone insane. But it was entirely Lucy's fault. She would never ever do as she was told. She would never ever accept that he knew best. And the whole situation was going to hell in a hand basket fast and he could blame himself for that because he should never have arranged to meet her in the first place. Why the hell did what had happened two years ago even *matter* to him?

So, she had lied to engage his sympathy and ensnare him, pretending to be younger and more innocent than she actually was. He already knew why she had done it. She had lied to impress him because he was rich and there was nothing more complex behind her behaviour back then than greed and a desire to rise in the world. He had been cunningly targeted and chased by hundreds of other women for the same reasons. Why was *her* deception still raw?

As he swung into the car, radiating blazing tension, his dazzling eyes splintered like green lightning with anger and Lucy stared at him.

'You still have a terrible temper,' she complained. 'And you just kidnapped me and the police did nothing—'

'Maybe you should've tried a little screaming and struggling to demonstrate fear,' Jax mocked, convinced that she was secretly delighted to be in his limo again and probably already planning a lucrative rehash of their Spanish fling.

No way, he swore to himself, black lashes almost hitting his cheekbones as he glanced studiously away from her, sitting there as she was watching him like a little spider planning an intricate web in which to capture him. On the other hand, *he* could play her the way she had once played him, he conceded grimly. And while he was doing that he could do whatever he wanted to do with her. That thought, that very idea took him aback because he didn't usually play games with women. But there was no denying that the concept of playing games with Lucy hugely turned him on.

Lucy breathed in slow and deep to calm herself. She focussed on the strong male thigh next to her own, the fine fabric of his trousers pulled taut across his powerful muscles and across his crotch. Her attention lingered there a split second longer and then hurriedly shifted because it was obvious that he was aroused. Why? Did he *ever* think of anything but sex? Colour warmed her cheeks because once they had had a very physical relationship. It had lasted six weeks, with them only becoming intimate in the last two, but during it she had realised that sex was unbelievably important to Jax and an unapologetic drive he made no attempt to restrain. Bella, after all, had been conceived in a brazen episode in a changing-room cubicle, she recalled in serious mortification. She had *tried* to say no but she had never been very good at denying Jax when her own body burned for his like a fire that couldn't be doused.

'I hate you,' she told him truthfully, still thinking about that changing-room cubicle in which the use of precautions hadn't figured.

'Because I found you out?' Jax drawled in a tone of boredom. 'Or because I dumped you?'

Lucy's nails bit crescents into the soft skin of her palms. She had told him the truth: she *did* hate him. In fact the idea of wreaking revenge on Jax energised her. He was so unbearably confident, sure of his every move in a way she had never been. He was clever, successful and rich. He was also worshipped like the Greek god he resembled by women more akin to groupies than anything else.

'Where are you taking me?' she demanded curtly.

'Why do you even want to talk to me? It's a bit late in the day, isn't it?'

'Is it?' Jax traded unfathomably, leaning forward to press a button that opened a gleaming bar.

'I don't understand you!' Lucy bit out in frustration.

'Why would you?'

Jax thrust a foaming glass of champagne into her hand, thoroughly disconcerting her. Big blue eyes skimmed up to his in confusion and she looked so lost and bewildered that a momentary pang of conscience pierced his tough hide. Of course it wasn't real, he recognised angrily.

Fool me once, shame on you, fool me twice, shame on me.

He knew he could trust Lucy to put in an award-winning performance. He would get what he wanted. He would get answers and doubtless tears, self-justification and grovelling into the bargain. He positively warmed to an image of Lucy grovelling and a smile flashed across his forbidding mouth. Lucy on her knees poised to please…just what the doctor would order for a bored billionaire.

That was what lay at the root of his bizarre behaviour, he reasoned broodingly. He was bored. Bored with the flattery of too many far too eager to please women. Well, Lucy had never been into the art of hanging off his every word and complimenting him on his brilliance. Lucy had fought him and criticised him and driven him crazy on many occasions. Yet he had only been with her six short weeks interspersed with the business trips that had parted them. Six weeks. That was a sobering acknowledgement. Why did he remember so much about her when generally he was challenged to recall the name of a woman he had shared a bed with only a week ago?

She had hurt his pride. That was why. That was the only reason he still remembered her, Jax decided. Well, that and the supercharged, highly satisfying sex...

Lucy sipped the champagne, bubbles bursting under her nose and tickling, tiny beads of moisture cooling her too hot face. She felt out of control and she didn't like it. She was in Jax's car and she didn't know where he was taking her or why he would want to talk to her after so long. She crossed her legs, then re-crossed them, looking everywhere but at him.

'I want to go home,' she said abruptly.

'No, you don't.'

'I don't trust you. I don't want to be anywhere alone with you,' she told him sharply.

'My housekeeper lives in,' Jax murmured flatly.

'Like that's going to change my mind!' Lucy scoffed. 'Nobody you employ will go up against you. Do you think I'm stupid?'

'A little hysterical,' Jax confided. 'And it's unde-served. I've never harmed you in any way.'

'But your employees will if you tell them to. I was

dragged off of *Sea Queen* two years ago and I got hurt,' Lucy told him reluctantly.

Jax turned his head to frown at her as the limousine coasted to a halt. 'What on earth are you talking about?' he demanded.

The door beside him clicked open and then the one beside her. She climbed out onto a well-lit driveway fronting an ultra-modern villa of quite astonishing size. The cool night air hit her hard and she felt slightly dizzy. A large glass of wine topped up by champagne had been too much for her system, she acknowledged heavily. Alcohol always hit her hard.

'We'll discuss this indoors,' Jax ground out impatiently. 'Come on...'

How had she got herself into this situation? Lucy asked herself with angry self-loathing. She didn't know where she was and had no idea how to get home again. She *should* have kicked up a major fuss when Jax had lifted her out of her chair at the bar but she had let him get away with it sooner than cause a public scene. In certain moods, Jax was as unstoppable as a juggernaut. He didn't care what anybody thought. The only opinion he cared for was his own.

'I want a taxi home,' she informed him. 'Right now...'

'I thought you were dying to tell me about the assault on the yacht,' Jax murmured, shooting her a politely enquiring appraisal that she immediately distrusted.

Lucy hovered uncertainly, noting the security team standing around and the older woman waiting to greet them at the front door. Compressing her lips, she forced herself to follow Jax, carefully picking her path up the steps into the contemporary hall. The preponderance of mirrors and multiple reflections confused her and she didn't object when Jax rested a light hand on her back to guide her into a huge reception room furnished with sofas and monochromatic modern art works.

'Assault...yacht,' Jax prodded expectantly. 'When did this happen?'

'About two weeks after I last saw you in Spain—'

'I had already left the country by then. Tell me what happened.'

'I went looking for you and I was told you weren't on board the *Sea Queen*—'

'Which was true.'

'The crew member that dealt with me was horrible. He called me names and manhandled me—'

Jax had fallen very still. 'In what way were you "manhandled"?'

'I said that I wasn't willing to leave until I was given a phone number or an address where I could contact you. Maybe that was foolish,' Lucy muttered ruefully. 'Anyway, this big bald guy got really aggressive and called me a whore and just dragged me across the deck and pushed me down the gangway. I fell at the foot, bloodied my knees and my elbows and nobody helped me. And someone had called the marina security to escort me away and they accused me of trespassing in a restricted area. It was hideous.'

A frown line had drawn his fine ebony brows together. 'I refuse to credit that any member of the crew would be so rough with a woman—'

Lucy bridled. 'Well, believe it…it happened!'

'Nor can I accept that there was verbal abuse. But I can confirm that you would not have been given my phone number or address because I left that instruction,' he admitted grimly.

'Why was that necessary? What did you think I was going to do?' Lucy framed in an angry rush. 'Spring a terrorist attack on you? Turn into a stalker?'

'I didn't want you making a nuisance of yourself,' Jax advanced flatly, turning away from her for an instant, memories interfering with his thoughts.

What she had made him feel had been too intense. In the aftermath of his discovery of her true nature, he had overreacted, he acknowledged with hindsight, stepping back and instinctively protecting himself from further exposure to her. It had seemed imperative that he neither speak to her nor see her again.

'I can't understand why you went to the yacht or why you tried to contact me again,' he said drily, swinging back to her with his brain fixed firmly in the present.

Bitter recriminations bubbled on Lucy's lips and

she swallowed them back because she didn't want to make an announcement about Bella in the midst of a heated dispute. And Jax might be poised in front of her as ice cool and expressionless as a glacier but the atmosphere felt combustible and the tension was horrendous.

'Obviously I tried to contact you...but you simply vanished. I didn't hear from you again. Most people would seek an explanation—'

'There was a *very* obvious explanation. I'd grown bored,' Jax murmured with derision.

'Sometimes you are a very nasty piece of work,' Lucy mumbled shakily, appalled that he could throw that humiliating statement in her face.

'Put your cards on the table, *koukla mou*. And maybe I will too.'

'I don't know what you're getting at—'

'Stop acting like a poor little victim—stop faking it,' Jax urged with stark impatience. 'You told me a lot of lies back then—'

'No, I didn't!' Lucy broke in furiously.

Exasperation gripped Jax. She was moving agitatedly round the room, luminous blue eyes fixed intently to him. The floor lamp behind her turned that pale dress almost transparent, clearly delineating the rounded swell of her small, succulent breasts and the shadowy outline of her pink areolae. He went hard, his reaction instantaneous.

'*What* lies?' Lucy demanded hotly, watching the

fluid movement of his long, lithe body as he paced the tiled floor in front of her.

He was so beautiful he still took her breath away. It wasn't merely his lean, strong face and stunning green eyes. Jax simply radiated masculine power from the aggressive angle of his arrogant head to the square swing of his wide shoulders and the decisive gait of his long, muscular legs. She was so busy staring, so busy drinking him in with greedy eyes that she couldn't concentrate. A prickling sensation assailed her nipples and tightened them into hard little nubs while a sliding, pulsing warmth began low in her pelvis.

'What lies?' she mumbled afresh, her brain in a fog.

Throbbing with arousal, Jax compressed his sculpted lips. He was done with conversation. Lucy would verbally twist and turn and prevaricate and embellish and evade until he was ready to strangle her. And why was he even bothering? He didn't ever travel an emotional road with women these days. He wasn't interested in their motivations and their deepest secrets. He kept it simple, straight. So, why wasn't he being straight with himself? He hadn't brought Lucy home to *talk* to her, had he? His mouth quirked into a flashing sardonic smile as he studied her.

It was the bad-boy smile Lucy had seen Jax wear a dozen times in glossy photos. It wasn't the smile that had once made her heart jump and fill to over-flowing with love. It was a dark edgy smile with a sensual hint of threat in it.

A forbidden tingle of anticipation infiltrated what remained of her defences. She took a sudden step back, struggling to keep her distance and stay in control. But Jax reached out a hand and closed it round hers in a sudden movement, pulling her to him before she could back off. He wrapped both arms round her, lifting her easily off her feet to hoist her high against him.

It was a decisive moment and she knew it, knew she should push her hands down on his shoulders to force him to put her down and release her. But nothing was ever that simple for Lucy when it came to Jax. As he brought her down he nuzzled against her neck, dark stubble scratching her tender skin, and a shudder of awareness powerful enough to leave her dizzy enveloped her. The scent of his cologne laced with clean, husky male flared her nostrils; he smelled so unbelievably good she wanted to bury her nose in his hair. Her hands went round his neck and for a split second as he worked his erotic path towards her parted lips she clung like a limpet.

Just one kiss, she bargained with herself, just *one*, but the man who had once seduced her with kisses had no intention of breaking his perfect track record. He always knew what she wanted and he gave it to her, all the seething passion he had ther,' Lucy swore breathlessly, unable to even make herself look at him.

Jax wanted to break something. Instead he breathed in very deep. Lucy hadn't changed. She had to have all the ducks in line before she would fire. Two years ago, that simple process of withholding sex had worked on him but he was no longer that suggestible, Jax told himself with fierce conviction. Yet when he touched her, she *owned* him, he recognised, unnerved by that realisation.

As she struggled with a singular lack of dignity or cool to refasten the difficult ties on her slender shoulders, Lucy's hatred of Jax rose like a tide of poison inside her. Ten seconds and he had had her half naked, nothing but a pair of knickers standing between her and total nudity. She had been a pushover. Maybe she was so starved of sex she *did* need a man in her life, she decided, her eyes stinging with hot, angry tears. But that man would not be Jax Antonakos.

'The limo will take you back home,' Jax told her flatly. 'That is if you *really* want to leave.'

'It's my turn to do the walking away,' Lucy framed gruffly, loathing coursing through her slight body in such powerful waves that she trembled with it. 'I wish I'd done it two years ago. What were you planning on happening? Another session of unprotected sex? Haven't you ever had consequences from that?'

taught her to crave. He kissed her and she went up
in flames. Her body flared into shocking awareness and suddenly burned back to almost painful
life with every plunging thrust of his tongue. She
gasped and quivered, filled with all the hunger she
had suppressed.

He brought her down on a firm but yielding surface and her head fell back as he wrenched down
her dress to squeeze a straining pink nipple between
his fingertips, swiftly following it up as she arched
up to him in response with the warm sucking pull
of his mouth. It was as if a river of liquid fire ran
down through her to engulf her feminine core. A
strangled moan of excitement was torn from her as
his mouth traced a fiery path down over her twisting body, long, lean fingers clenching on a slender thigh.

And just then she wondered how he had contrived that skin-to-skin contact and the answer
shook her so much that she yanked herself violently free and rolled off the sofa, hitting her hip
painfully hard in the fall. Her dress fell round her
knees. Tears of pain and mortification in her eyes,
she got onto her knees and, with great difficulty,
clumsily and awkwardly hauled her dress back up
over her exposed body, shame roaring through her
in long agonising waves.

'*Thee mou...*' Jax began rawly.

'I want a taxi home. This is not going any fur-

'What the hell are you trying to imply?' Jax demanded in a raw undertone.

Lucy flung her head back, all fired up on adrenalin and resentment and bitterness. 'When you got bored and dumped me,' she told him shakily, 'you left me pregnant—'

CHAPTER FOUR

JAX HAD FALLEN very still. 'That's not possible—'

'Why? Are you infertile?' Lucy shot back at him, unimpressed. 'I don't think so because we have a *child*, Jax. A little girl, who's fifteen months old.'

Jax stared back at her in rampant disbelief, hard lines settling between his nose and mouth, his handsome bone structure drawn stark and taut. 'Impossible,' he said again, green eyes brilliant with outraged denial.

'That last week we were together you had sex with me in a changing-room cubicle and you didn't take precautions,' Lucy reminded him angrily. 'Why do you think I tried so hard to get in touch with you that I got thrown off the yacht? I needed help.'

Shock ensured that Jax's brain continued to rebel and tell him that what she was saying was totally and absolutely impossible but his memory was infinitely more accurate. He knew he had taken that risk and had thought nothing of it at the time, indeed revelling in the reality that not even the thin layer of a condom separated him from her. He also realised in that moment that if she was telling him the truth, he had very probably made the biggest, messiest mistake of his life.

Panic hurtled through Lucy when she saw the shrewd dawning of genuine concern in his glittering green eyes. What had she done? Throwing it at him like that? Oh, my goodness, what had she done? Dully she recognised that she had been hitting back at him the only way she knew how. Needing to shock and hurt him as he had once shocked and hurt her with his rejection. But she knew instantly that she should not have used Bella like a weapon against him.

'This has to be discussed,' Jax intoned in a driven undertone.

'Not tonight. I want to go home,' Lucy breathed tightly. 'Right now.'

'You can't tell me I could be a father and then—'

'Yes, I can,' Lucy incised fiercely. 'I can do whatever I like just as you do whatever you like. And it's not a question of "*could* be a father". Bella is yours because I've never been with anyone else!'

Jax knew that was a lie for he had seen her cheat on him with his own eyes but DNA testing would provide proof neither of them could refute. He was appalled by the idea that he could have unwittingly had a child with a woman who not only lied and cheated but also had a criminal record. Even his parents' numerous unsuccessful marriages and affairs paled beside such a development. And the existence of an illegitimate Antonakos heir would send his father through the roof.

'I want to see the child,' Jax told her doggedly.

Lucy lost all her hectic colour. 'No.'

'If that child is half mine, you don't get to say no. I'll call in the family legal team,' Jax warned her without skipping a beat. 'Who looks after her when you're at work?'

That reference to lawyers and the reality that she was a working mum made a cold, hollow sensation of fear spread inside Lucy's tummy. 'My stepmother,' she told him, struggling to suppress the defiance rising inside her because a mood of conciliation struck her as being far more sensible in the circumstances.

'I'll call in with you tomorrow and we'll take care of the necessities,' Jax breathed coldly as he strode out to the hall. 'I need your address—'

'No.' The sense of being trapped built up inside Lucy until she felt almost suffocated by it. She had told him about Bella. She had done it in a recklessly provocative way too, absolutely the worst way to give Jax bad news. As volatile as he was, he didn't need the encouragement. And she had no doubt at all that learning that he was a father was very bad news on his terms because from the instant the concept had set in, Jax had turned icy-cold and businesslike.

Now, however, Lucy recognised that she had to deal with the fallout from her impulsive decision and that would entail finally telling Kreon and Iola the truth.

'If you come in the morning I'll be there,' Lucy conceded abruptly. 'I usually only work evenings. My father and stepmother have a funeral to attend, so they won't be at home.'

Jax demanded the address and then stood poised in the doorway of his home watching her clamber into the limousine outside. Lucy tore her gaze from his forbidding stance and told herself that she had only done what had had to be done. He had the right to know about Bella. It was his own fault that he hadn't found out about his daughter sooner. Maybe he wouldn't want anything to do with their child, Lucy reasoned with sudden hope that that might be the case. And then she felt horribly guilty because she knew how much it hurt not to have a father and she didn't want her daughter to suffer the same way.

Yet when she looked back to her affair with Jax she could never have believed that they would have ended up so bitterly opposed. That night after the yacht party, Jax had sought her out and insisted on seeing her back to her room at the bar.

'You *are* over twenty-one?' he had checked. 'I don't get involved with anyone younger than that.'

'I'm twenty-three,' Lucy had lied instantly, adding on four years to her age, determined to make that all important grade for him.

He had told her he would pick her up for dinner the following evening. She had told him she was working.

'Take a night off,' Jax had urged.

'I can't afford to,' she had argued.

'I'll cover the cost of it,' Jax had declared.

'But then you'd be paying for my time and I couldn't agree to that—'

'You're very difficult,' Jax had condemned.

'And you don't understand how to take no for an answer.'

'I want to see you again,' Jax had proclaimed impatiently.

'I'm free Thursday night.'

'I don't want to wait that long.'

'All right. You can see me at midnight tomorrow when I finish my shift…unless that's too late for you?'

'No, that will do.'

'But know upfront I'm not spending the night with you, so if that's what you're expecting, just forget about me,' she had warned him staunchly.

Lucy had learned to be blunt with men. She thought of it as managing their expectations. She had gone out with so many men who had simply assumed that she would sleep with them at the end of the night and who had reacted badly to a refusal. But her body was the one element in her world that Lucy had always felt was truly hers and until she finally met someone who could make her want him enough to move beyond that she had no intention of sharing her body with anyone. She genuinely hadn't expected Jax to be any different and she had slowly learned her mistake until saying no to Jax had become painful because she hadn't been able to control her own hunger.

'You're too defensive. Not every guy is out to nail you—'

'You mean you're *not*?' Lucy had exclaimed in surprise.

'I can see that trying to be smooth and seductive with you will be a huge challenge,' Jax had laughed, flashing her a highly amused smile.

And she had started falling for him that very night because that glorious charismatic smile of his had stopped her in her tracks and left her short of breath. She had met him the following night, sharing tapas and a couple of drinks with him in an upmarket bar. But sadly, she had dropped off to sleep in the middle of the conversation, bone tired from being on her feet serving all day. He had shaken her awake and taken her home without even attempting to kiss her, confiding that yawns weren't sexy. He had put his phone number in her phone while she slept and the next day he began texting her, first letting her know that he would be out of the country for a couple of days, then arranging to see her on her next free night.

A day later Kat Valtinos had shown up at the bar

and cornered her. 'Jax is the ultimate playboy and you're the British equivalent of trailer trash—'

'Probably,' Lucy had conceded, looking back on her troubled poverty-stricken past.

'Obviously Jax will get bored fast and you look like the clingy sort.'

'I haven't had a chance to cling yet but I'm a quick learner. Does he like clingy women?' Lucy had asked, wide-eyed. 'Is he your boyfriend?'

'No, a very good friend,' Kat had declared. 'But you're wasting your time. I intend to marry him.'

'Tell that to him, not to me,' Lucy had advised and got back to work, ignoring the bitchy brunette until she'd finally stalked out in a snit at not being taken seriously.

The following morning, Lucy rose early after a sleepless night of wandering painfully through her mortifyingly fresh memories of being with Jax two years earlier. She watched her father and stepmother leave to attend the funeral. Over breakfast they had been too preoccupied with a sad and affectionate exchange of stories about their now deceased friend to notice how heavy-eyed and silent Lucy was.

But Lucy was also restless with anxiety and operating on pure adrenalin. Now that Jax knew about Bella she had to worry about how he would act on that information. She winced at the knowledge that Jax had power over her again. Certainly he had rights as a father that she could not deny. But would he choose to exercise those rights and seek an active parenting role?

Barely an hour later, Lucy received her first taste of Jax choosing to exercise his rights. A smartly dressed, fast-speaking lawyer arrived and asked her to agree to DNA testing and no sooner had she given consent, her face burning at the humiliating suspicion that Jax could doubt that he had fathered her child, than a lab technician arrived and took samples. That matter dealt with, the lawyer then settled a confidentiality agreement down in front of her. It seemed to be what Lucy had seen referred to as a 'gagging order' in the media and she refused to sign it, sticking to her guns when the older man persisted in his persuasions.

'Mr Antonakos does not like what I shall describe as private matters broadcast in the public domain. If you sign this document, it will form a secure basis for good relations between you in the future.'

'I can assure you that I have no intention of speaking to the press but I'm not prepared to sign anything that says I cannot talk about my own daughter,' she told him quietly.

By the time the older man departed, Lucy fully understood that he had been engaged in a potential damage-limitation plan. And Lucy was utterly unnerved by Jax acting to protect himself and the reputation of the Antonakos family even before he had definitive proof that her child was his. She was appalled that he could distrust her so much that he suspected that she might sell nasty stories about him to the newspapers.

In truth she did have a very low opinion of Jax but she had every intention of keeping that low opinion to herself for her daughter's sake. Whatever else Jax was, he was and always would be her daughter's father and she didn't want to do anything to damage that relationship. That meant, she registered with a sinking heart, that she would have to keep her personal feelings very much to herself. Airing her anger, resentment and bitterness would be destructive and the situation they were in where they shared a child but nothing else would be difficult enough to deal with.

An hour after the lawyer departed, Jax arrived and, for once, not in a limousine. He roared up outside on a motorbike and it was only as he doffed his helmet on the way to the front door that she realised it was him and not someone making a delivery. He was trying to be discreet, endeavouring to ensure that he wasn't recognised, she realised. When she had first met Jax in Spain he had only recently stepped into his late brother's role and as he had been relatively unknown there had been no paparazzi following him around then. Now that a kind of celebrity madness erupted around Jax's every public appearance she was grateful that he was being care-

ful because she did not want to see her face or her
daughter's appearing in articles full of embarrassing speculations.

Lucy opened the front door and stepped back. Jax
strode in, bringing with him the scent of fresh air,
leather and masculinity. In the narrow hall, he tow-
ered over her and she thrust the door quickly shut
to walk into the spacious front room, which was
sprinkled with colourful toys and baby equipment.

Jax slung his motorbike helmet down on a chair
and raked impatient fingers through his black hair.
'Where is she?' he demanded.

'Bella's having a nap. I'll get her up in ten minutes. She wakes very early in the morning and then
she gets tired again...' Realising that she was gab-
bling, Lucy flushed, insanely conscious of Jax's
stare.

Lucy sported cropped jeans, a pink tee shirt and
bare feet. She looked very young and cute and definitely hadn't dressed up for his benefit. Jax was ir-
ritated that she had not made the effort. He hadn't
slept much the night before. The cold shower hadn't
worked any miracle and that sexual tension piled on
top of the shocking announcement Lucy had made
had done nothing to help. When he had a problem
Jax liked a plan to work towards, a plan with firm
boundaries. Unhappily there was no convenient plan
available to tell him how a man behaved when he discovered he was a father even though he had never

wanted that particular joy. But he *had* been reck-
less with Lucy in the birth-control department and
in retrospect he could not forgive or excuse himself for that lack of responsibility. Of course, he reminded himself wryly, the kid might not be his, in
which case he was dealing with nothing more than
a storm in a teacup.

'Stop staring at me,' Lucy told him, cheeks burning from the intensity of his scrutiny.

'Of course I'm staring. You dropped a bomb on
me last night. I'm still reeling,' Jax breathed in a raw
undertone, green eyes glittering warily below curling ebony lashes.

'Well, I've been mentally reeling from the minute
I discovered I was pregnant,' Lucy confided truthfully. 'With time you get used to the idea. I couldn't
bear to imagine life without Bella now.'

Jax scanned the youthful glow of her unblemished
skin and the luxuriant tumble of strawberry-blonde
ringlets that merely highlighted her bright blue eyes.
He acknowledged her beauty for there was no denying what was right in front of him. As his body began
to react he clenched his teeth together hard and wandered back towards the front door, determined not
to let his libido take over when there would soon be
a child in the room.

'Coffee?' Lucy pressed as the awkward silence
stretched when he reappeared in the doorway.

'This is not a social visit,' Jax answered.

A cry sounded out somewhere above them and Lucy scurried upstairs, her face flushed by his deflating statement.

Jax plonked himself down on a sofa and struggled to relax but it had been more years than he cared to recall since he had been around a baby. He was godfather to several but his role had never been hands-on, nor would it ever have been more because nobody expected a single man, who was also erroneously known as his actress mother's only child, to be comfortable dealing with young children. Ironically Jax had learned the daily routine of how to look after a baby when he was only twelve years old. It had been the end of the summer before his mother had finally engaged a nanny because Jax was returning to boarding school.

He heard the creak of the stairs and vaulted upright. As he straightened his shoulders Lucy walked into the lounge and he immediately saw the child in her arms. He froze into a statue in the same moment that he saw the little girl's black curly hair and the green eyes. That fast, that dramatically, Jax knew he didn't need a DNA test to prove to anyone that the little girl was his. Lucy's child was the living image of his kid sister, Tina, and that uncanny resemblance hit him like an avalanche. His mother had had very strong genes, he reckoned ruefully, for both he and the little sister who had died as a toddler had looked far more like Mariana than the men who had fathered her two children. He knew too that his striking likeness to his mother had only been another nail in his coffin as far as his oversensitive father was concerned.

'This is Bella...' Lucy framed, kneeling down to settle the little girl gently on the floor.

A thumb planted in her rosebud mouth, Bella studied Jax fixedly, her green eyes full of curiosity.

Jax bent down and lifted a toy that broke straight into a catchy tune as soon as he pressed the right button. Bella grinned and came closer, steadying herself on one powerful thigh with a clutching little hand.

'She's not scared,' Jax remarked, marvelling that he could still speak normally after being plunged without warning into some of his darkest memories. The remnants of that guilt, anger and pain still resonated powerfully with him.

'No, she's quite confident and she likes men. My father makes a fuss of her and spoils her. I suppose we all spoil her a bit,' Lucy conceded, staring at the little tableau of Jax and his daughter as they each assessed the other. 'She looks very like you—'

Jax skated a teasing forefinger off Bella's determined little chin and swallowed thickly, struggling to master his almost overwhelming emotions. He should not cloud his first meeting with his daughter with such tragic memories, he censured himself fiercely. The past was the past and it would be wiser to leave the sad little ghost of Tina safely buried there.

'What is it?' Lucy prompted, troubled by the feverish glitter of Jax's stunning eyes, their brilliance enhanced by the surround of spiky black lashes. 'What's wrong?'

'Nothing,' Jax insisted, his wide sensual mouth slashing into a sudden forced smile, for he had shared far too much private stuff with Lucy in the past and he had no plans to make himself vulnerable in that way again 'But when she was born you should have moved heaven and earth to ensure that I knew I was a father.'

Unprepared for that criticism when she had tried every way she knew how to contact him, Lucy stiffened. 'That's not fair—'

'What isn't fair,' Jax fielded as he accepted the little plastic doll that Bella brought him, 'is that this little girl and I weren't able to be in each other's lives from the start.'

Lucy's bright blue eyes hardened. 'As you said though, when you dumped me, you didn't want me making a *nuisance* of myself,' she reminded him thinly. 'If you didn't want to hear from me ever again, how was I supposed to tell you?'

Not trusting himself to speak in the mood he was in, Jax shrugged a muscular shoulder in brooding silence.

'Didn't think you'd have an answer for that,' Lucy

sniped, leaning down to clasp Bella's hand and guide her into the kitchen where she set about filling a toddler cup with milk.

Bella pushed against the back door, keen to get out onto the patio and play. Lucy opened it and watched her daughter toddle out into the sunlight to retrieve the little plastic pram she loved.

His child, *his* daughter, a new generation in the Antonakos family, Jax acknowledged, watching Bella swig her milk and then set down the cup with exaggerated care before pushing the little pram out onto the small lawn. Somehow, he didn't know how, he didn't care, Lucy *should* have contacted him, he thought angrily.

'I have missed out on over a year of my daughter's life,' Jax intoned grimly. 'That is not acceptable—'

Under sudden attack, Lucy spun. 'No, what was unacceptable back then was the way you treated me!' she condemned with spirit.

Jax thought about the contents of the investigative file he had been given. He saw no point in throwing the contents of that file in Lucy's face now. Likewise her little session in that alleyway. His reaction had been all too human. He had let his anger and aggression take over and dictate his moves. 'I'm afraid it never occurred to me that you could be pregnant,' he admitted in a harsh undertone. 'I should've acknowledged that possibility and made provision for it but I didn't. That was a serious oversight on my part.'

A little of the tension in Lucy's slender shoulders eased. 'Yes, it was.'

'Then let us not waste time stating the obvious and rehashing a past we both prefer to forget,' Jax countered impatiently.

'We can't forget it when Bella was born from it,' Lucy argued helplessly. 'We may not like each other but we'll just have to live with that. I'll make coffee, and not because this is a social occasion but because we need to learn how to act civilised.'

As Lucy left the doorway to switch on the kettle Jax strode out onto the patio, unable to let his newly discovered daughter out of his sight and reach. It crossed his mind that he had no intention of living with his distaste of Lucy and forging a civilised alliance with her as a co-parent. With what he knew about her past, he didn't, *couldn't* possibly trust her to be a caring decent mother. Bella's well-being came first and nobody would ever persuade him that his child could be safe with a mother who had once dealt in drugs and sold her body. It didn't matter that to all intents and purposes Lucy appeared to have turned over a new leaf.

Jax, after all, was the son of a drug addict. He had heard too many promises, seen all too many fresh starts *and* witnessed the subsequent falls from grace. Bella would always be at risk of harm if she remained with her mother, he decided cynically. He would have to fight Lucy through the courts for custody of their daughter. He was sure that she loved Bella to the best of her ability but with her fatal weakness for substance abuse he couldn't trust her to always put their daughter's needs first.

'Are we capable of behaving like friends?' Lucy asked Jax hopefully as she hovered in the doorway.

Jax glanced at her in astonishment, questioning how she contrived to still look so young and innocent in spite of her misspent past. Friends? Never, he conceded wryly. And once Lucy received the first official communication from the Antonakos legal team and realised what he planned to do friendship would be the last thing on her mind. But what other choice did he have?

'You have to stop blaming me for everything that's gone wrong,' Lucy told him squarely. 'In any relationship it takes two people to screw up. Remember that…'

As she spoke Bella fell flat on her face on the lawn and let out a yell, followed by frantic sobbing. Jax strode across a flower bed and snatched the little girl up into his arms, speaking softly to her, smoothing a lean brown hand gently over her shaking back to soothe her before getting down on his knees to show her something on the ground in the clear hope of distracting her from the fright she had sustained. Lucy stared at that seemingly effortless display of child management in sheer amazement, involuntarily impressed.

'Jax...' she muttered in a daze.

Once Bella was restored to calm again, Jax set her down. His lean, strong face taut, he glanced at Lucy, noting how the sunshine lit up the shades of red in her hair and illuminated her perfect skin. Lucy bent to pick up the pram and the shapely curve of her heart-shaped derriere pulled tight below the cropped jeans she wore. Jax remembered ripping her jeans off her, desperate to sink into the damp, welcoming heat of her, and fierce tension gripped him as he suppressed the hunger flaring through him like a dangerous burning brand. 'In a couple of days I'd like to take Bella out. I'll bring a nanny with me if that keeps you happy.'

'I assumed you would be waiting for the DNA results before you did anything official,' Lucy parried, thoroughly disconcerted by his request as she walked back to him.

'The DNA tests will only confirm what I already know,' Jax murmured. 'Are you going to make me fight for access to her?'

Lucy winced and set her teeth together. If in doubt, weigh in with the threats. That was Jax. He could afford the very best lawyers. Ultimately he would be entitled to time with his daughter whatever she did or said and trying to ignore that reality would be foolish. In any case, didn't she want Bella to have a father? Yes, she did, but she hadn't expected to have to share her time with her daughter quite so immediately.

'No, but I wouldn't want her away from me for more than a couple of hours at a time,' she admitted. 'She's still very young.'

'I can agree to that,' Jax traded. 'Give me your phone number and I'll be in touch.'

Bella cuddled to her, Lucy watched Jax swing back onto the motorbike, the lithe powerful lines of his big muscular body moulded by his designer jeans and leather jacket. Across the road a car started up and pulled out to follow him, his security team, she assumed.

When her father and stepmother returned from the funeral, Lucy sat them down and finally told them the truth.

Straight away her father erupted like a raging volcano. '*Jax Antonakos?* Are you serious?'

'Please don't get mad,' Lucy pleaded. 'It will only make this situation worse.'

'You were only nineteen, Lucy,' her father protested with pained condemnation. 'He must be nearly ten years older than you!'

'Well, he can't be blamed for that. When he said I had to be over twenty-one to spend time with him I lied,' she admitted ruefully. 'I said I was twenty-three—'

'You *lied* to him?' Kreon repeated censoriously.

'Calm down, Kreon,' Iola interposed gently. 'She was a typical teenager and when a handsome young man approached her, she pretended to be older and more sophisticated than she was. A lot of girls that age would have done the same thing.'

'Yes,' Lucy admitted, her cheeks burning.

Iola dragged the rest of the story of those six weeks in Spain from Lucy while Kreon sat fuming, his anger unhidden. 'I knew his father, you know,' he told them abruptly. 'And he was a selfish, arrogant thug of a man too.'

'Jax's father? You *knew* him? *How?*' Lucy asked, astonished by that admission.

'My parents worked for the family of Heracles Antonakos's first wife, Sofia, in London. Sofia and I grew up together and we never lost that friendship even though she lived in a very different world. She was only thirty when she died,' Kreon revealed gruffly.

'I'm really sorry I didn't tell you the truth from the start,' Lucy confessed. 'I didn't want to upset you—'

'Never you mind about me being upset,' Kreon told her through compressed lips. 'Be grateful I'm here to support you. Antonakos sending in the lawyers straight off is your first warning of his plans—'

'What do you mean?' Iola interjected worriedly.

'Well, was what happened this morning a nice or considerate thing to do to the mother of your child? Demanding DNA testing? Trying to browbeat Lucy into signing a confidentiality agreement? As a first warning shot, it tells us all we need to know…'

'Jax is trying to protect himself. I can't blame

him for that,' Lucy muttered ruefully, troubled by her father's angry gravity and all too conscious that she was the cause of the lines of stress that had appeared on his weathered face.

'He can protect himself all he likes but not at your expense or Bella's,' Kreon replied.

Lucy was anxious and preoccupied when she went into work that evening and she struggled to remember the drinks orders and deliver them back to the correct tables. Her father's genuine fear of what Jax might be planning had seriously scared her. Not for the first time she wished she had the ability to get inside Jax's head.

Earlier that day he had been strangely distant with her but very different in his wholehearted response to Bella. In retrospect it was hard to credit that he had been kissing her, *touching* her only the night before. Of course, that made sense, she told herself squarely. Everything had changed the minute she'd told Jax about their daughter. She recalled his glacier cool when she had first told him at his house and barely restrained a shiver of apprehension. Her father's concern had set off all her internal alarms and had left her on the edge of panic and thinking thoughts she had believed she would never think again…

What if she simply upped sticks and vanished? She had done it before and she could do it again. But it would be wrong, her inner voice warned her sternly. It would be wrong not to give Jax the opportunity to form a relationship with his daughter. It would be equally wrong for Lucy to run away from the life her father and stepmother had generously offered her. Running away from her problems would be the childish thing to do and she wasn't a child any more...

CHAPTER FIVE

'So, you are Lucy's father,' Jax commented, lounging back against his office desk with lethal cool, not a shade of what he was thinking revealed by his lean, darkly handsome features. 'Where were you all the years Lucy was growing up in the care system?'

Kreon straightened his shoulders. 'That's my business and Lucy's. She's welcome to tell you if she wants. But I'm here now to protect the welfare of my daughter and my granddaughter.'

'I don't understand how you plan to do that,' Jax remarked.

'Oh, that's very simple,' Kreon told him almost cheerfully. 'I have access to secrets that your father would kill to keep out of the newspapers—'

Taken aback, Jax laughed. 'My father fears nothing. Is this some sort of clumsy blackmail attempt? I advise you to back off now before I call the police.'

'That will be your decision but it won't stop me sharing your family secrets with the press. In fact having me arrested will only add legitimacy to my claims,' Kreon pointed out calmly. 'Your father hates me. I will tell you that for free. But why do you think he leaves me alone? He is afraid of what I might know.'

'You're talking a lot of nonsense and I don't intend to listen to it,' Jax told him, crossing the room to open the door and hasten the older man's departure.

'Your brother, Argo, wasn't your brother because he wasn't your father's child,' Kreon delivered very softly. 'I think Heracles only found that out *after* your brother died and, believe me, he does not want that humiliating truth spread across the newspapers.'

Jax froze, shock washing over him in an almost physical attack that pulled his every muscle taut to breaking point. In a driven movement he thrust the door shut again and swung violently round.

'What do you want?' he demanded of the smaller man, refusing to think of what he had just been told, refusing to join the dots and acknowledge how well that revelation would dovetail with his own quite recent miraculous change of status within the Antonakos family.

'In return for my continuing silence, I want you to marry Lucy.'

Jax stared back at him in savage disbelief. '*Marry...* her?'

'She was a teenager when you wrecked her life. You owe her the security of a wedding ring. It doesn't have to be a life sentence for either of you. But it would give her and Bella the safe harbour and the recognition they need to have a better life—'

'She *wasn't* a teenager!' Jax raked back at him in furious rebuttal.

'Lucy was twenty-one last month. We celebrated with dinner at that hotel where she works.' Kreon shot him a sourly amused appraisal. 'My wife tells me that teenaged girls do lie about their age occasionally.'

'Twenty-one,' Jax repeated thickly, fighting to master the violent anger lashing through him and a powerful urge to strangle Lucy for having dared to lie to him. 'I would require proof of those allegations about my brother, Argo.'

And from an inside pocket Kreon produced a handwritten letter which he handed to Jax. It had been written and sent to Kreon when his father's first wife, Sofia, was terminally ill. Unable to face death with such a weight on her conscience, Sofia had admitted the affair that had led to Argo's conception, although she had not named her lover.

'Why didn't you come forward with this at the time of her death?' Jax demanded harshly a few minutes later. 'With this letter, you were in possession of facts that were unknown to everyone else involved.'

'Sofia couldn't have thought through what she was doing. Your father had just lost his wife and Argo had lost his mother and her letter would have destroyed them both. Back then Heracles had no idea that Argo wasn't his son. What do you think he would have done?' Kreon grimaced. 'He would've disinherited the boy and cast him off.'

Jax stared at the wall, knowing that there was a fair chance his father would have reacted like that in the first heat of his fury. Once Sofia had let that genie out of the bottle there would have been no putting it back.

'I didn't want that responsibility. I'm not a cruel man. It was a secret that shouldn't have been told. I never liked your father and he was a lousy absentee husband but, fond as I was of Sofia, once she was gone I preferred to mind my own business…that is, until an Antonakos threatened the security of my own flesh and blood.'

Long after Kreon had gone, Jax studied the copy of the letter the older man had allowed him to keep. He was still shaken even though the woman had died long before he was born. The contents of that letter would distress his father, although, like Kreon, Jax was inclined to believe that somewhere around the time of Argo's death his father had found out that his eldest son was not actually his son. That would better explain why Heracles had found it possible to move on so fast from that loss and adjust his attitude to Jax almost overnight.

That new knowledge and understanding just about ripped Jax apart, not to mention his view of his family. He had looked up to the big brother he had never really got to know very well and he loved his father. And why *did* he love Heracles, who had proved to be a useless parent when Jax was young and in need of a father? Ultimately, he had recognised that the older man deeply regretted allowing his dented ego and workaholic ways to triumph over the ties of blood. Heracles was hopeless when it came to expressing emotion though and Jax had realised that he suffered from the same flaw. His father had stumbled on blindly after Mariana's infidelity had made him a laughing stock in the media, protecting himself as best he could by avoiding his ex-wife…and unhappily that avoidance had included Jax.

Jax hadn't really thought about how he actually felt about Heracles until that moment, but when he thought of his father being forced to see the tragedy of his first marriage spread across the newspapers he knew he couldn't allow that to happen. Sofia had died after a long drawn-out fight against breast cancer. Heracles was domineering and manipulative and interfering but he had once adored his first wife and the son he had believed to be his.

Jax's first act was to summon Zenas and tell his security chief that he wanted an in-depth private investigation carried out on Kreon Thiarkis and his daughter, Lucy. How the hell had something as basic as Lucy's age been wrong in that file? Her parentage

had been incorrectly recorded as well. Lucy *did* have
a Greek father. What else could also be wrong? He
needed the background and facts he could rely on. He
also needed to check out Kreon's ties to his father's
first wife, Sofia. And to his father. After all, it was
his father who had sent that file to him.

Jax began to mull over the other things he had
learned. Lucy was still only twenty-one years old?
And had been only nineteen when they had first
met? Memories swirled in a colourful haze in Jax's
head and he marvelled that he had not recognised
Lucy's immaturity for what it was. She had been impulsive, outspoken, naïve and unnervingly ignorant
about facts he took for granted and a sneaky little
unrepentant liar...*obviously*.

And no way was he prepared to marry her! Kreon
could not blackmail him into doing what he had
never wanted to do, he assured himself stubbornly.
On the other hand, Jax also knew he could not stand
back and watch his father endure the scandal that
would blow up if Kreon went to the press to sell his
story. People would enjoy reading about the skele-
tons hidden in the Antonakos cupboard and his father would lose his dignity. At the age of seventy,
Heracles deserved to keep his dignity, Jax decided
heavily. He might have been a lousy husband in Kreon's eyes but he had surely not deserved the tragic
conclusion to his first marriage. Knowing how badly
Heracles had reacted to his own mother's infidelity,

Jax could hardly begin to imagine what his father must have felt once he realised that Argo was not his child. Surely Heracles had suffered enough for being a less than stellar husband? How dared Kreon Thiarkis threaten him?

Yet even in the grip of that seething Antonakos rage, Jax could still not stop planning. He knew that it was up to him to control the situation. He reached the stage of listing pros and cons. Were he to marry Lucy, he would get her back into his bed. A sliver of raw anticipation raked through Jax's tense, angry body and he recognised that that was a fringe benefit that he would very much enjoy. At the same time he would also gain a stronger legal right to his daughter and he would not have to fight to gain access to her.

Nevertheless, Jax hated being told what to do and Kreon Thiarkis had just thrown a double whammy at him that came attached to a very high price tag. Primarily he was in a rage because he knew that Kreon had given him a choice but it was the hateful choice of picking between the lesser of two evils: marriage or his aging father's public humiliation. He could tell Kreon to do his worst and then stand by and watch his father get hurt. Unfortunately, family loyalty and a very real affection for his inadequate father warred against that option. But the alternative was to surrender his freedom.

No more hot and cold running women, no more

sexually self-indulgent variety in the bedroom. But
then that wasn't quite true, Jax allowed with a sudden strong sense of relief. Even Kreon didn't expect
him to stay married to Lucy for ever. Kreon was expecting an eventual divorce, which would still leave
Lucy and Bella respectfully acknowledged as mem-
bers of the Antonakos family and financially secure.
Thee mou…he could do marriage on a short-term,
strictly temporary basis, particularly with Lucy playing the starring role in his bed every night. Furthermore, Bella would have his name and the safeguard
of his presence in her daily life. But just how was
he expected to cope with a father-in-law he wanted
to strike down and kill in cold blood?

As an Antonakos, Jax had little experience of
being threatened. He was too rich, too powerful to
cross and his father had long enjoyed the same protection. But Kreon was in legal possession of very
private and personal information that went right to
the heart of Jax's family, the kind of secret nobody
wanted exposed and picked over in public. Even
worse, one revelation would almost inevitably lead to
others. What might be dug up about his own mother?
Jax shuddered at the prospect of Mariana's drug-
addicted frailties and Tina's death being dragged out
into the punishing light of day. At that point it struck
him that a wedding ring was a worthwhile sacrifice
if it bought peace and left the family's dirty laun-
dry untouched.

* * *

Lucy studied the text from Jax with wide incredulous eyes. He had asked her when she finished work.

I'll pick you up when you finish and we'll talk.

Jax? *Talk?* Jax had been known to leave the room or remember a pressing engagement when any form of serious discussion was threatened. Jax didn't believe in talking about stuff. He thought in private and then he acted to fix a problem. He didn't share the reasoning that led to the decision. He believed that talking only heightened the wrong emotions, encouraged divisive stances and made issues seem worse than they were. When she had once tried to talk to him about where their affair was heading he had become angry and he had walked away. Naturally he had, she conceded, because he had known their affair was going nowhere.

But obviously he had to talk to her about Bella, she reasoned ruefully. Even he couldn't make unilateral decisions about the daughter they now had to share. He would want to make arrangements to see Bella again, he would want to ask questions about what the little girl liked and didn't like. That he was prepared to talk was a healthy sign, Lucy told herself heavily, striving to muster some enthusiasm about the idea of sharing her daughter with her father.

Before she even went into work, her own father

had lectured her, urging her not to do to Bella what had been done to her. She had grown up without a father because her mother had selfishly chosen not to tell Kreon he had a daughter. Now, quite unnecessarily, Kreon was advising Lucy to take a long-term view and keep her anger and resentment out of the situation.

'I know it's a big ask,' Kreon had conceded, 'but you have to deal with what's happening now and handle it sensibly. Try to concentrate on what's best for Bella.'

Her father's outlook had surprised Lucy because he seemed to have come to terms with what she had told him about Jax very quickly and had now taken a more detached view of events. Unfortunately everything still felt painfully personal to Lucy. Jax had rejected her but he had *not* rejected their daughter. She knew she shouldn't be thinking that way but she couldn't help it because she was only human.

A car picked her up from the hotel. It wasn't a limo and Jax wasn't in it but she recognised Jax's security guards. She climbed in, smoothed down her denim skirt and worried at her lower lip with the edge of her teeth. She was wondering what Jax wanted while telling herself to keep her temper and her daughter's emotional and physical well-being at the forefront of her mind regardless of what he might say.

Jax had plans as well. He would not confront Lucy

about anything until they were safely married. Hopefully by then he would also know how accurate that file he had actually was. But he was also well aware of how deceptive Lucy could be, he reminded himself grimly, thinking of the familiar flash of that red dress below the street lights as she'd walked down that alleyway to have sex with another man. Lucy wasn't the faithful type. Two of his father's three wives had betrayed him with other men and Jax's own mother had never been faithful to anyone. Surrounded from childhood by broken, dishonest relationships, Jax had always tried to avoid emotional involvement and commitment. But when his daughter came into the equation he discovered that he badly wanted to give Bella the storybook family he had never had. Something better, something happier, something lasting…

Lucy walked dry-mouthed and nervous into the house with the confusing mirrored hall. The elegant drawing room looked more welcoming than it had on her last visit with only a couple of lamps lit to leave the rest of the very large room shrouded in shadow. When Jax stepped out of the shadows, she flinched and stilled on the threshold.

'I ordered supper for you.' Jax indicated the table spread with a selection of snacks.

Jax wore jeans and an open-necked shirt. He shouldn't have taken her breath away in such ordinary garments but he did. The jeans clung to his narrow hips and outlined his long, powerful thighs. The pale shirt accentuated his bronzed skin tone and the blue black of his hair. She sucked in a breath in the tense silence and clashed with shimmering green eyes fringed by black and her heart hammered out a drumbeat inside her.

'Supper,' she repeated, that being the last thing she had expected from him, but she stepped fully into the room to head for the table, grateful to have something other than Jax to focus on.

'Help yourself,' he advised.

Settling down on a sofa, Lucy needed no further encouragement because she was always hungry after work and she was involuntarily impressed that he had remembered that little fact. She filled a plate and poured a cup of tea. 'This is what I call civilised,' she admitted with a wry smile.

'I thought it would be,' Jax said. 'Were you working in that outfit?'

Lucy smoothed a self-conscious hand over her comfy skirt with which she had teamed a black tee shirt. 'Yes...'

Jax gritted his teeth. A tripwire stood in front of him but he neatly avoided it by refusing to give way to his inner caveman. The short skirt showed off her surprisingly long and very shapely legs and the tee shirt shaped her pert breasts to perfection. Once upon a time he had objected to her wearing the sort of clothing that revealed her body and that had set off heated arguments. Now he was respecting boundaries to preserve the peace. He sank down onto the sofa opposite her while mentally trying to come up with garments that would still be fashionable but which would miraculously shield that glorious body from the visual attention of other men. And he finally registered that there were no such garments on the market. Lucy had always outshone her clothing. From her bright tumbling hair to her luminous skin and radiant blue eyes, Lucy glowed with sheer energy, attracting attention even in a crowded room.

'It's not a short skirt,' Lucy remarked, knowing his flaws.

'No, it's not,' Jax agreed, wishing she hadn't directed his attention to her pale slender thighs and knees because it only made him think about the sheer glory of parting them. Furiously conscious of his growing desire, Jax rocked forward, his lean, strong face taut, green eyes semi screened by his lashes.

'You said you wanted to talk.' Lucy widened her eyes suspiciously. 'Was that a joke?'

'No…' Silence fell while Lucy munched through her third sandwich. 'We have a dilemma and I have come up with a solution,' he spelled out in a roughened undertone as the tip of her tongue chased a crumb from the corner of her mouth.

'Bella isn't a dilemma. She isn't and never will be a problem,' Lucy assured him quietly. 'I'm not going to be difficult about you seeing her or anything like that.'

Jax breathed in deep, striving to make himself get to the point and bite the bullet. 'If we married, we would be in a position to give Bella far more.'

Lucy put down her sandwich unfinished. *'Married?'* she repeated in consternation. 'But you don't ever want to get married.'

'I didn't plan to have a child either,' Jax reminded her. 'But Bella is here now and that changes the whole picture. I want to give her what I didn't have. A mother, a father and a settled home, all the security that only a traditional family structure can give her.'

Lucy was stunned because she had never dreamt that she would live to hear Jax admit a desire to embrace such conventional ideas. 'Neither of us had that,' she conceded unevenly. 'But life isn't perfect and that's the way it is—'

'But we *can* change that,' Jax sliced in forcefully. 'We don't have to live apart when we could raise Bella together, as a married couple.'

Lucy blinked rapidly, her heart in her mouth, her feet flexing because nervous tension made her want to get up and walk round the room. 'Together?' she repeated in bewilderment.

'We can get married and make a home for our daughter, the kind of home neither of us had the advantage of growing up in,' Jax extended with unearthly calm.

'I don't know much about your background. Well, I know your parents divorced when you were young but—'

Jax stiffened. 'You already know that my mother was unstable and not a reliable parent. Men came and went in her life. None of them ever stayed. She was too high maintenance. I don't want our daughter to have to adapt to that kind of lifestyle.'

'With respect,' Lucy said uncomfortably, 'I'm not a world-famous, gorgeous actress and I don't think my lifestyle and your mother's would have anything in common.'

Jax released his breath in a small hiss of frustration. 'Do you really believe that your life is going to stay the same now that I know you are raising my daughter?' he pressed in disbelief. 'Do you honestly believe that you can go on working as a waitress and living with your father? Obviously I will take care of all your expenses now—'

'No,' Lucy broke in with a frown. 'I don't want that.'

'But that's what will happen whether you like it or not. Naturally I want my daughter to enjoy the same lifestyle that I enjoy myself and I can't believe that you would deny her what she is entitled to receive. Bella is an Antonakos,' Jax reminded her with pride.

'Yes but…' Lucy's voice ran out of steam as she began to think about everything he had said.

He was asking her to marry him. Jax Antonakos

was asking *her* to marry him, offering her the dream conclusion she had once secretly cherished and then buried deep two years earlier. For the space of several frantic minutes Lucy could only stare down into her tea and struggle to come to terms with a proposal she had never expected to receive. A home, two parents and a real family for Bella. That truly was the ultimate ideal for Lucy when it came to her daughter. Her mother had ended up alone raising Lucy and Lucy had ended up alone in the care system because the authorities had failed to trace Kreon. Sometimes she hated herself for making the same mistake with Bella and having to bring her up without a father.

'Are you serious about this?' Lucy asked breathlessly.

'Of course,' Jax asserted levelly.

'But you *never* wanted to get married,' Lucy reminded him helplessly.

'And then Bella came along and turned everything upside down,' Jax confessed with complete honesty. 'This is no longer only about you and me. We have to think about our daughter and about what would make *her* happy.'

'Unhappily married parents wouldn't help,' Lucy pointed out apologetically.

'I see no reason why we shouldn't make a go of it. Even sitting here having a serious conversation I can barely keep my hands off you,' Jax admitted bluntly, his stunning green gaze glittering across her heart-shaped face and watching the flush of awareness slowly build there. 'And if you're honest, it's the same for you.'

Lucy dragged her attention from his sleek, darkly beautiful features with the greatest difficulty. But trying to blank her mind, trying not to look at him was no use when the hunger inside her felt like an insidious virus that refused to die. And she knew what the cure was and that unnerved her. The only cure she knew was the wild, pounding plunge of his body into hers and the explosive release he would give her. And even that wasn't a permanent fix, she thought shamefacedly. She had once craved him as she craved air to breathe. She set her tea down with a jarring crack on the coffee table, her hand trembling.

'Look at me,' Jax urged, breaking the smouldering silence.

And Lucy looked even though she knew she shouldn't, desire clawing at her insides, awakening the yearning buried deep within her body. A ragged breath escaped her, her pulses racing. Her breasts ached but the biggest ache of all was between her legs, at the very heart of her where she was burning with need. That voracious need that hungered for his touch terrified her because it was so ready to rage out of control and sweep all restraint and all common sense before it.

'We're getting married as soon as it can be arranged,' Jax decreed.

Her head flew up. 'You can't just—'

'One of us needs to be decisive. You want to bury your head in the sand and run away from the responsibility.'

'No, I don't.'

'We do it for Bella. Together we make a family,' Jax intoned.

'It's not that simple.'

'Nothing worth having is ever easily acquired,' Jax said drily. 'Everything worthwhile I have ever achieved has come at a cost and there have always been sacrifices involved. Are you willing to make sacrifices for Bella's benefit?'

Lucy leapt upright in frustration. 'Jax! Stop trying to railroad me!'

'In a couple of days the paparazzi will be on to us. I want to pre-empt them with a wedding, a big splashy wedding, which they won't be expecting,' he told her grimly. 'They'll be happy enough to settle for wedding photos.'

'Do you really *want* to do this?' Lucy whispered shakily.

'I want you. I want my daughter. To give her what we both want, to give her what she *deserves*, we have to get married,' Jax countered with measured cool. 'I can handle that. Can you?'

And Lucy thought about that, really seriously thought about that even though her brain did not feel up to that challenge. Even when she had dreamt about marrying Jax two years earlier she had known it was only a dream because Jax had seen too many relationships break down to have any faith in the marriage bond. He had admitted that to her in Spain and afterwards he had seemed unnerved by what he had told her and he had cut their evening short.

'We will fight,' Jax forecast. 'But we're good at making up again.'

Lucy flushed and nodded jerkily and he laughed huskily for they had always ended up in bed after arguments, taking refuge in the sexual unity that bridged their differences.

'And if you don't want to give up work after we're married I'll make a special arrangement for you,' Jax murmured lazily. 'I'll buy a bar and I will be the *only* customer and you can serve me to your heart's content.'

'You say the craziest things,' Lucy muttered, shaking her head while locked to the stunning green eyes gleaming below his black lashes.

'I will say whatever I have to say to get that ring on your finger,' Jax admitted truthfully. 'The world's your oyster tonight, *koukla mou.*'

But Jax was no perfect pearl for her to acquire, she thought helplessly. Jax was complicated and reserved and unpredictable. Living with Jax would not be easy; it would be a roller coaster of highs and lows. Yet didn't she want to take the chance? It was a chance she had never thought she would have. Yes,

Jax had treated her badly in the past but marriage was an equal partnership and this time around she wouldn't have to surrender her independence or her self-respect because money wouldn't be an issue. Giving her daughter the secure and loving childhood she had not had herself would mean so much to her. How could she refuse that offer?

'I'll marry you,' Lucy breathed tautly. 'But you'd better not make me regret it.'

Thinking of the secrets he had withheld and the complete honesty that he would eventually have to practise, Jax breathed in deep. He had given way to blackmail to protect his family but in marrying, he acknowledged grimly, he would be protecting his new family from potential harm as well.

'I should be honest,' Lucy murmured, her blue eyes awash with regret and apology. 'I don't trust you.'

Jax, who had learned never to trust anyone, particularly one's nearest and dearest, almost laughed out loud. Lucy would flourish like a tropical flower in the Antonakos family.

CHAPTER SIX

EVEN A FEW days before the wedding Lucy still couldn't quite accept that she was getting married. She was very tense and stressed. Jax had insisted on picking up the bill for the hundreds of guests invited and her father had been dismayed to discover that he was only allowed to cover his daughter's more personal expenses. In the same way Jax had organised the church and the venue for the reception.

And he had done all of that from a safe distance, leaving Lucy to handle her father's hurt pride and angry complaints. Jax, after all, was the man who had never planned to marry and since the moment Lucy had agreed to marry him Jax had come no closer to the centre of bridal activity than a phone call because he had hired a wedding planner to take care of everything. Lucy had had the freedom to make her own choices but had relied heavily on the planner's advice because she knew nothing about high-society weddings. Her brain was still stuffed,

however, with the turmoil of selecting flowers, colour schemes and table arrangements from frighteningly long lists of options and having to discuss
every possibility.

Iola had gone shopping with Lucy for a dress and
Jax had been allowed no input there. Lucy had gone
for lace and a fancy pleated train that would be re-
movable if she was dancing and she had picked the
sweetest little outfit for Bella.

It was ironic that Jax had pretty much vanished
as soon as she'd accepted his proposal and that had
really annoyed Lucy. He had said that he had too
much work to get through and he had only visited the
house once when she had insisted he come and meet
her father and her stepmother. That had been a very
awkward hour of stilted conversation, she recalled
ruefully. Jax had been very cool and polite and her
father had been stiff and formal. Iola and Lucy's efforts to lighten the atmosphere had made little difference. It had been painfully obvious to Lucy that
her father and her bridegroom didn't much like the
look of each other.

And then there was the troubling question of her
future father-in-law, Heracles Antonakos.

Lucy had assumed that Jax's father would want to
meet her in advance but apparently not, and Jax did
not seem to know whether or not his father would
attend their wedding, an admission that had made
her wince. Obviously, Heracles Antonakos was not

impressed by his son's decision to marry a waitress and he wanted nothing to do with the event. But Jax refused to be drawn on the sensitive subject and had urged her to be patient.

'It's a delivery…for you,' Iola called up the stairs to Lucy.

Lucy clattered downstairs and signed for the package she was given, turning it over and back before walking into the kitchen to open it. She extracted a letter and a small jewellery box and frowned.

'Is it a wedding present?' Iola asked.

'No…it's from some woman called Polly, who *says* she's one of my sisters,' Lucy whispered in deep shock, reading the closely typed lines to learn that her mother had only passed away a few years before at a hospice and commenting on the fact to Iola.

'I always assumed that Mum had died when I was a child…possibly during the three years I was adopted because of course I wouldn't have been told about it then,' Lucy confided. 'But according to my sisters they too only found out about her death afterwards because she didn't want to see any of us while she was so ill. But she left us all rings given to her by our fathers…and it was only then that my sisters found out that I existed.'

'Strange,' Iola commented. 'But if she was very ill, possibly she wasn't thinking very clearly. Is there a ring in that box?'

Lucy opened the box and extracted a small ruby

ring with a smile. 'It's very pretty. I'll wear it when I get married. It's wonderful to have something that my mother actually wore,' she murmured with a sad look in her eyes.

'Read the rest of the letter,' her stepmother urged. 'Tell me about your sisters.'

Unfortunately Polly didn't offer much information beyond the fact that she was married and had children just like Lucy's other sister, Ellie, who was a doctor. What she did say was that she and Ellie very much wanted to meet Lucy and get to know her.

'She couldn't have chosen a worse time to contact me,' Lucy mumbled, settling down to read the letter again. 'She hasn't given me an address or anything but she has given me a phone number, which I could use to talk to her.'

'You could invite your sisters to your wedding,' Iola suggested.

Lucy grimaced. 'No. I don't know them and I don't think Polly knows I'm a mother as well either. It would all be too awkward for a first meeting and in any case they would need more warning than a few days to attend. I'll call her as soon as we get back from our honeymoon. But my goodness, this is exciting,' she muttered abstractedly. 'I wonder what Polly and Ellie are like. Do I look like them? Do you think they have the same father?'

Kreon walked in and Lucy handed him the letter straight away to read. He stared down at the ring on the table and then he lifted it. 'I gave this to Annabel as an engagement ring. It's not a real ruby, you know, but it looks well. It was all I could afford at the time—'

Lucy laughed and removed it from his hand. 'I will still wear it with pride, Dad.'

'You have your mother's bright and beautiful smile,' Kreon told her fondly. 'But you have a kindness as well, which she never had.'

'Maybe I inherited that from you,' Lucy replied, watching her daughter hug her grandfather's knees and raise her arms to be lifted with all the confidence of a child who knew she could always expect a welcome.

Lucy couldn't sleep that night. Jax phoned and she told him about Polly's letter. It shook her that her most driving instinct was to share that very private news with Jax even when he wasn't around. But then Jax knew better than most about complex family divisions, she reasoned, shying away from the inner awareness that she trusted Jax more and wanted to share everything with him more than she was willing to admit.

Jax urged her to do nothing until he had checked out her sisters and she got cross with him then and told him to mind his own business. Not that he could do anything else, she conceded, when there wasn't enough personal information in that letter to allow Lucy or indeed Jax to identify either of her sisters or even work out where they lived. Polly had kept the

letter short and sweet as a first approach and Lucy's
mind buzzed with conjecture about the siblings she
had never met.

Some of her excitement gradually subsided, however, when she thought about Ellie being an actual
doctor. Ellie was obviously very well-educated and
clever and possibly Polly was as well. Lucy could
well be the odd one out, the lesser sister, the odd-
ball who didn't fit in. That idea troubled Lucy because it seemed to her that that was the story of her
entire life: never quite fitting in anywhere. Not with
her mother, not in the foster homes, not even in the
short-lived adoption she had enjoyed until her adoptive parents died in a car crash and she was sent back
into care. And she hadn't fitted in with Jax either,
had she? He had dumped her and walked away without a backward glance. Yet now, he was marrying
her. How did that make sense?

He was only marrying her for Bella's benefit,
she reminded herself, feeling her pride sting and
her heart sink at that awareness. Could their desire
to do well by their daughter be enough to sustain a
marriage? Lucy didn't want make-believe and she
didn't believe in perfect. She believed that she had realistic expectations. But she did desperately *want* to
have a real marriage and be part of a proper family.
It was what she had dreamt of all her life and never
managed to achieve. Now that Jax was offering her
that opportunity she planned to make the most of it.

The morning of the wedding dawned bright and sunny and, having done her hair and her make-up for herself, Lucy donned her gown. It was a perfect fit, swirling round her in delicate shimmering white lace. As a mother she had felt self-conscious about wearing white but she hadn't felt the need to make a statement either by choosing another colour. In any case she was marrying the man who had become her first lover and the father of her daughter and she wasn't ashamed of either fact.

A heaving bunch of paparazzi waited behind crash barriers outside the vast Metropolitan Cathedral in the city where the Greek Orthodox ceremony was being held. Lucy was unnerved by the questions shouted and the flash of cameras and she gripped her father's arm tightly as they negotiated the shallow steps and moved below the arches into the church.

'Royalty once got married here,' Kreon murmured with satisfaction. 'I never dreamt that one day I would see my own child taking her vows below this roof.'

The comment lightened Lucy's tension as nothing else could have done. 'Glad I've finally done something to make you proud but why are the paparazzi so interested?'

'You are about to become a member of one of the foremost families in Greece. Naturally, the public want to know who has captured the notorious playboy, Jax Antonakos—'

'I wouldn't say captured is the right word,' Lucy muttered uncomfortably as they paused at the end of the aisle and her father shook out her small train for her and offered his arm to her again with a proud smile.

'He's a very fortunate man. I hope he appreciates that. You look really beautiful,' the older man declared with satisfaction.

Tears stung the backs of Lucy's eyes because she was touched by her father's faith in her. She watched Jax turn his handsome dark head and look at her and the ability to breathe died in her throat. The closer she drew to him on their slow walk down the aisle, the more gorgeous he appeared, his dramatic green eyes welded to her approach. Colour warmed her cheeks and tingling heat surged low in her pelvis. She felt as if all her dreams were coming true in that moment and she scolded herself for being too emotional and sentimental. Jax was neither sentimental nor romantic. He didn't love her and she didn't love him, she reminded herself firmly, but they had Bella to bind them and, in time, maybe they would find that more than their daughter kept them together.

Jax studied Lucy with heavily lidded eyes, his attention roaming over every exquisite shapely inch of her petite body. The gown was a triumph, a delicate lace affair of simple design that enhanced her slight stature and gave her elegance. He didn't look to see how his father was reacting. Only minutes earlier he had noticed his father's absorption in Bella where she sat on Iola's knee across the aisle. Heracles longed for grandchildren, and the knowledge that he had a little granddaughter he had yet to meet had at the very last minute made him decide to attend the wedding. True, Jax wasn't expecting his father to be in a party mood because Heracles hated Kreon Thiarkis and hated that his son was marrying Kreon's daughter, but Jax was relieved that Heracles had put family first and shelved his reservations to share their day.

Some of the ceremony went over Lucy's head, for which she blamed Jax, who had said he was too busy to attend a rehearsal at the cathedral when the services of an interpreter had been available. She concentrated on the simple Greek words that she knew and smiled nervously up at Jax when he slid the ring onto her finger. Their eyes met and the burn inside her spread like wild fire. It was utterly inappropriate but she had never wanted so badly to be kissed. Jax angled his arrogant dark head back and gave her a teasing smile of naked challenge and she went for it as she had always gone for it when he egged her on. She stretched up awkwardly in her very high heels, her hands clutching at his arms to steady herself, and *still* she wasn't tall enough.

With a husky sound of sensual amusement, Jax gathered her up and raised her to his level to taste her lush parted lips for himself. And for a split second, Lucy forgot everything. She forgot that she was in public, she forgot the guests shifting in their seats and the imposing robed Archbishop who had conducted the service. The taste of Jax's mouth was like a shaft of sunlight bursting inside her after a long winter. It charged her up, rendered her helpless with longing, and the plunge of his tongue into the moist interior of her mouth only multiplied the explosive effect of that kiss on her body. Her heart hammered, her pulses raced as Jax slowly slid her down his lean, powerful frame to stand on her own feet again.

She caught a glimpse of Iola's grin and just as suddenly appreciated that she was still in public view. A swoosh of mortified pink lit up her heart-shaped face as Jax closed his hand over hers and walked her back down the aisle.

Jax was amazed that he felt so relaxed. He had expected to loathe every minute of the wedding. Knowing he was protecting his father was one thing, doing what had to be done when it went against his own instincts was another. But that hot little taste of Lucy's passion assuaged those feelings. She wanted him, she wanted him just as much as he wanted her, and for the moment that was as much consolation for his sacrifice of freedom as he needed.

He had struggled against anger, resentment and bitterness throughout the two weeks it had taken to set up the wedding. He had kept his distance from Lucy because he was afraid that she would guess that he was not the enthusiastic bridegroom he was purporting to be. Deception of any kind had always been a challenge for Jax. He was very talented at keeping his feelings to himself but he was very bad at *faking* anything. He had found the drinks engagement with Kreon and Iola extremely uncomfortable and Lucy's demands for his opinion on the colour of the bridal flowers and such nonsense had simply exasperated him. For two solid weeks, Jax had rigorously reminded himself that he was acquiring Lucy and his daughter and protecting his father by getting married. But even that couldn't disperse the sour flavour of having to do what he had always sworn he would not do and take a wife.

Outside the cathedral the paparazzi went into a frenzy of excitement when the bride and groom appeared. Jax's father stalked silently from cathedral to limousine without pause. It was ironic that Heracles was furious with his son for marrying Lucy. Only after Jax had pointed out that he had had a daughter with Lucy had Heracles gone from raging to dark muttering, finally accepting that a waitress, who was also the daughter of an obnoxious criminal, was entering the Antonakos family. And having learned about that criminal record, Jax had not argued in his father-in-law's favour. Agreeing that Kreon was obnoxious had somewhat soothed his father's ire.

Jax had been tempted to bring up the file he had been given on Lucy two years earlier but he had decided to take a rain check on that line of enquiry until after the wedding. Getting information about Kreon Thiarkis had been surprisingly easy but getting information on Lucy was proving deeply problematic. She had lived in so many different places and had even been adopted at one stage when her name had been changed. Indeed the discovery of just how grim Lucy's growing years had been had saddened Jax. Some years after the adoption she had gone back to using the name she had been given at birth. But Lucy's frequent childhood moves read like a depressing indictment of social services care and the investigator striving to trace her movements during her adolescence was currently at an admitted standstill.

Of course, you could simply ask her for the details, Jax reminded himself wryly. Could he trust her answers? Or would she lie to mislead him, hoping to cover up conduct she might now be ashamed of? Jax needed the confidence of knowing that he had the *whole* truth. Naturally he expected her to deny the drugs offences but, so far, no official record of any such offences had been found. Was it possible that the detective agency his father had used had confused Lucy's identity with someone else's? Was it even remotely possible that she was innocent of the charges in that file? But then hadn't he been equally shocked when he'd seen her with that man in the alleyway? Lucy didn't wear her sins or her flaws on her lovely face.

With the ease of long practice Jax buried the

memory of Lucy's betrayal deep where he didn't have to think about it. If he thought about it, he mused grimly, it would drive him off the edge, the way it had two years ago when he had tried to find solace in the bottom of a bottle: the aftershocks of giving up Lucy had been little short of terrifying for a male who needed to stay in emotional control. For a short while he had been overpowered by his conflicting feelings, not something he was willing to recall or relive. In fact even remembering that made him flinch.

They arrived at the hotel and settled down with Bella in a private room set aside for their use to drink champagne and await the arrival of their guests. Poised by the window, Jax tensed. 'That's my father's car arriving. Come on. I want to introduce you and Bella.'

By the time Jax and Lucy reached the grand foyer, however, Iola and Kreon were already greeting Heracles. And then there was one of those strange little moments of absolute stillness as Kreon said something and Heracles backed up and then suddenly lurched forward and punched the younger man with angry ferocity. Lucy was aghast when the fight broke out. Her father responded, lurching clumsily after Heracles to return that punch and then receiving yet another for his pains, for Heracles was very fit and fast on his feet for his age. Further violence was only forestalled by the Antonakos bodyguards who stood between the two men to keep them apart. Heracles let out an angry roar of frustration.

'Stay back,' Jax warned Lucy, striding in to intervene and grip his father by both his arms to restrain him, since it was obvious that none of their staff had the nerve to lay actual hands on their irate employer.

All red in the face and still patently desperate for a fight, Heracles roared something angry in Greek. Jax stole a glimpse at the guests piling through the entrance doors and then stopping dead to stare at the spectacle and he suppressed a groan. He said something to his father and shepherded him over to a door of the private room. Pushing open the door, he gestured to Lucy's father to follow him. Looking reluctant but red-faced and more than a little embarrassed, Kreon finally did so. Jax was trying to sort the argument out, Lucy recognised ruefully while wondering what Heracles Antonakos had against her father that had so overpowered his manners.

'Men!' Iola proclaimed dramatically at her elbow, making Lucy emit a startled laugh. 'Thank heaven, Jax got them out of sight.'

'What sparked off that punch?' Lucy demanded in bewilderment.

'Apparently Kreon and Jax's father have some past history. Kreon didn't go into detail but it's obvious that Jax's father hates him and almost didn't come to his son's wedding because he knew Kreon would be here.' Iola rolled her eyes. 'Don't let it spoil your day.'

'I shan't,' Lucy responded, stroking Bella's curls distractedly while thinking that family relations promised to be taxing with their fathers at odds.

With Iola by her side, Lucy welcomed guests and chatted until she saw Heracles and Kreon emerge again together with drinks in their hands and actually speaking to each other. But when Jax strode back to join her, raw tension was still stamped on his lean, darkly handsome features.

'Evidently you're quite successful in the peacemaker stakes,' Lucy remarked as he steered her into the function room to take their seats, mercifully moving her right before she had to greet Kat Valtinos, who looked ravishing in a cutaway emerald dress teamed with feathers in her hair.

'No, they achieved that without any help from me. I only stayed to ensure that hostilities didn't break out again,' Jax admitted. 'You still haven't met my father and I need to explain what happened out there.'

'Don't break the habit of a lifetime and tell me something,' Lucy urged with helpless sarcasm.

'It's not something I want to talk about but I must,' Jax breathed stiffly. 'However, it's old history and nothing to do with us. No doubt you're wondering why my father went for yours…'

'Kreon does seem to be an acquired taste with some people.'

'This is not a teasing matter,' Jax censured.

As she settled down beside him at the top table

Lucy was watching Heracles Antonakos make their daughter's acquaintance. Bella was fearless and she stared up at the older man and handed him her stuffed rabbit. Heracles's craggy face broke into a sudden unexpected smile and he sat down with Iola by his side and accepted the rabbit to make it walk across the seat beside him. Bella started to giggle and clutched at the leg of his trousers to stay upright.

'He likes Bella,' Lucy noted with satisfaction, willing to overlook and forgive a great deal if her daughter was accepted and appreciated.

'He loves children.' Jax fell broodingly silent and she glanced curiously at his lean, taut profile, help-lessly admiring the classic perfection of it. 'My father discovered after my brother, Argo, died that he could not have been his child. Argo needed a transfusion after the attack and I suspect it was discovered in the minutes before he died that he did not share my father's or my rare blood group.'

Lucy's eyes widened because she was completely disconcerted by that bombshell. 'My goodness, Her-acles must have been devastated to find that out—'

'Particularly as he idolised his first wife and de-spised my mother...and me...for my mother's infi-delity. When he found out that he hadn't fathered Argo he immediately suspected your father because of the close friendship Kreon had had with Sofia.'

Lucy winced. 'I honestly don't think it was that sort of friendship.'

'It wasn't. Kreon saw Sofia as a little sister. His mother, your grandmother on Kreon's side, was Sofia's nanny and as children Kreon and Sofia spent a lot of time together,' Jax told her. 'Unfortunately having married Sofia my father distrusted their friendship and became jealous.'

'In other words, your father is an old dinosaur who can't credit that a man and a woman can have a platonic friendship,' Lucy commented, still watching Heracles as he lifted Bella onto his knee with careful hands.

'I wouldn't appreciate my wife being that friendly with another man either,' Jax admitted.

'Sadly I don't currently have any close male friends to torment you with.' Lucy sighed with unhidden regret on that score.

'You're a little witch,' Jax growled, running his forefinger along the lush line of her full lower lip. 'Why does that make me want to kiss you again?'

'You love a challenge?' Lucy whispered unevenly, meeting those stunning green eyes in a head-on clash and feeling more than a little dizzy with excitement, her lips parting.

'But I don't enjoy an audience,' Jax countered, running a finger back and forth across the delicate bones of her wrist below the level of the table.

Lucy was breathing in rapid shallow little gusts, insanely conscious of her body responding to him on every level. She could feel her breasts full and constricted within the bodice of her dress, her distended nipples pushing hard against the scratchy lace of her bra and then there was the tight locked-down tension and heat between her thighs, not to mention the dulled little throb there that made her ache and stiffen her posture.

'It's showtime—but not for what we want,' Jax murmured drily as Iola took a seat beside him and Heracles settled down beside Lucy with Bella still on his knee.

'She's very cute,' Heracles said of her daughter. 'She knows what she wants.'

'Mum... Mum,' Bella framed, lurching straight off Jax's father into her mother's arms and flopping down sleepily.

'She needs a nap,' Lucy sighed.

'Where's the nanny I hired for the day?' Jax asked.

The older woman was already approaching Lucy, ready to take the tired toddler off her hands, but Lucy stood up. 'I'll come upstairs with you and get her settled.'

'Your bride doesn't take hints, does she?' Heracles remarked with some amusement to his son. 'You'll have your hands full with the two of them.'

Jax, who very much wanted to follow his bride upstairs and have her settle *him* down, grimaced. 'I know it.'

'Well, you can't make worse choices than I did.

I won't say anything more,' his father declared piously. 'With my track record, I can't afford to preach, can I?'

'No, you can't.'

'Three marriages ending in one death and two divorces and your mother was almost as bad. We didn't set you much of an example, did we?' Heracles sighed heavily. 'By the way, I've set up the island for your honeymoon—'

Thoroughly taken aback, Jax frowned. 'But you live on Tifnos,' Jax objected, because he had been planning to take Lucy cruising round the Mediterranean on the yacht.

'Tifnos is yours now that you're a father. It was built to be a family home and I'm tired of living there alone in that great barn of a house. I've signed it over to you and I'm in the process of buying an estate outside Athens,' the older man told him in a tone of finality. 'It's time for me to step back and make room for the next generation.'

CHAPTER SEVEN

LUCY CAME OUT of the room where she had left the nanny watching over Bella and smiled at the sight of Kreon waiting for her. 'Dad? What are you doing up here?' she asked with a grin. 'Are you trying to escape all the polite chit-chat? Or have you heard a rumour that the food's going to be bad?'

Kreon shifted uneasily on his feet, his face grave and troubled. 'I have done something wrong and it concerns you.'

'What on earth are you talking about?' Lucy laughed as he urged her into an alcove with seats.

'Talking to Heracles made me see stuff...differently.' Her father selected his words with an air of discomfiture as he sat down. 'It made me appreciate that we've all had our tragedies and our triumphs but it's how we deal with them that makes us who we are. I'd like to be proud of who I am but right now I'm *not*.'

Lucy narrowed her eyes in confusion. 'You don't sound like yourself.'

'Jax's father neglected Jax because he despised Jax's mother, whom he divorced. He knows he can never make it up to Jax and he has to live with it every day, knowing that all those years he left his boy to deal alone with a very difficult woman,' Kreon told her.

'But you and I have a different history,' Lucy reasoned, tucking that fresh information about Jax into her memory to take out and ponder at a more suitable time. 'You didn't even know that my mother was pregnant when you left London and she didn't tell you later when she could have done—'

'That's not what I'm talking about,' Kreon told her heavily. 'For many years I hated Heracles Antonakos because he put me down over my friendship with his wife. I'm ashamed to admit that I took my resentment out on his son.'

Lucy's smooth brow had furrowed. 'In what way?'

'When Sofia was dying, she had a letter sent to me in which she confessed her darkest secret. She didn't have the nerve to tell her husband so she told me instead.' Kreon drew a crumpled envelope from his pocket and passed it to her. 'Give it to Jax, let him decide what to do with it now. In it Sofia confesses to having an affair and she admits that Jax's brother wasn't fathered by Heracles. I went to see Jax a couple of weeks ago and I threatened to take that letter to the newspapers.'

'Good grief...why would you threaten to do

something so horrible?' Lucy demanded in total disbelief.

'I wanted Jax to marry you and take care of you and Bella. I thought he owed you that security and I *still* believe that he does but coercing him into doing it was wrong and unjust. He was protecting his father from more heartache and I shouldn't have put him in that position. He is not responsible for his father's mistakes.'

Lucy had turned very pale and her stomach was curdling as if she had eaten something that disagreed with her. She studied her father in slowly dawning horror and comprehension. 'Are you telling me that you blackmailed Jax into proposing to me?'

As Kreon gave a guilty nod of silent confirmation, Lucy felt as though the bottom had just dropped out of her world. She stared at the brand-new wedding ring on her finger and felt sick. Jax hadn't wanted to marry her. No, he had been *forced* to marry her. It was ghastly. She looked at her father in stricken condemnation. 'Were you insane? I mean, what on earth could persuade you that *that* was an acceptable way to behave towards Bella's father?'

'I was angry with him. I wanted to punish Jax for seducing and abandoning you. It's not an excuse but at the time I honestly believed I was doing what was best for you and my granddaughter.'

'Because Jax is rich and powerful,' Lucy slotted in sickly. 'And now you feel bad about it because you've realised that rich and powerful people like Heracles Antonakos make mistakes and suffer just like everyone else.'

Kreon sighed. 'That's probably it in a nutshell. When I listened to Heracles talking I felt my anger draining away. He was a workaholic who neglected all his wives. But he came to the wedding today even though he didn't approve of you because he was making an effort to be supportive of Jax as a father should. That was the *right* kind of effort to make for a child, mine was wrong. What did I do today? I made a sarcastic comment and provoked that punch.'

'I'm really upset,' Lucy admitted, breathing in deep and slow to calm herself down. 'You'd better go back down and join the guests before Iola starts wondering where you are.'

'I'm sorry, Lucy. I've just felt so powerless since you came into my life. You had had such a rough time and I genuinely *did* want to make your life better,' Kreon confessed before he walked away.

And she understood exactly where her father was coming from *but* he had blackmailed Jax. Nausea stirred in Lucy's tummy. Jax, who would hold a grudge beyond the grave. Jax, who idolised the father who had ignored him for so many years, had been vulnerable. A deep sense of anguish flooded Lucy and an even deeper sense of shame. The father she had so easily come to love had let her down badly and shown her his feet of clay. That hurt as well. Was she always going to be a rotten judge of character?

But what did she do now? Well, the middle of a wedding didn't seem the ideal venue in which to open a very difficult conversation with Jax. Oh, by the way, my father mentioned that he blackmailed you... Lucy cringed and winced and hurt all over again. She hurt for her father and for Jax and for Bella, for surely the chances of such a marriage working out looked very poor. But most of all, she was discovering that she hurt for herself. Jax's apparent desire to marry her had filled her with hope and even unleashed a few dreams.

Only now it was obvious that Jax hadn't actually experienced *any* desire to put a ring on her finger. Her father had used the nastiest form of persuasion available to get that wedding ring on her hand. Hadn't it ever occurred to Kreon that it would be his daughter who had to deal with the aftermath of what he had done? Hadn't he appreciated how angry and aggrieved Jax would feel? Lucy shivered, suddenly feeling very alone and without support. She couldn't depend on her father and now it was equally obvious that she could not depend on her new husband either.

For the first time she badly wanted to speak to the sisters she had never met. It was crazy but she wanted to reach out and see if she could connect with a sister as she so obviously had failed to connect with

Jax or her father. Kreon had lied when he said that she could trust him. And Jax hadn't meant all those fine things he had said about how they could be a couple creating a secure family in which to raise a child. He had been forced to talk like that to convince Lucy to agree to marry him and she groaned out loud, remembering how unusually understated Jax had been that evening. She had already put her sister's phone number into her mobile for fear that she might mislay Polly's letter and she dug her phone out of her small ornamental bag.

She got a bad case of cold feet while the phone was ringing and almost stopped the call before it connected. And then it was answered by this sunny, confidence-inducing female voice and Lucy froze.

'It's Lucy…er…your sister…if that's you, Polly,' she gabbled in an uneasy rush.

'Lucy!' Polly proclaimed warmly. 'I'm so very happy to hear from you. Do you have any idea how long Ellie and I have been trying to trace you?'

'Why were you trying?' Lucy asked in genuine puzzlement.

'Because you're our sister and part of our family. Ellie and I always had each other but until recently I know you had no one. Of course, I appreciate that you have your father now—'

'That hasn't worked out so well,' Lucy mumbled in some embarrassment.

'I'm really sorry to hear that. Are you all right, Lucy?' Polly prompted anxiously.

Lucy stared stonily at the wall, hot prickly tears stinging the backs of her aching eyes. 'Well, not so great today...to be brutally honest,' she framed chokily.

'You sound upset,' Polly remarked with care. 'Naturally I don't want to pry but—'

'I'm not upset,' Lucy insisted chokingly. 'It's my wedding day—'

'My wedding day wasn't great either,' Polly told her ruefully. 'I assume the ceremony has already taken place? Do you love the man you married?'

It was a simple question but it froze Lucy from head to toe. She started to shiver, feeling cold and clammy. 'No, we're not in love. We got married because we have a daughter...at least I *thought* that's why we got married but seems I was wrong about that too,' she mumbled shakily.

'I can't believe you're already a mother at only twenty-one,' Polly exclaimed. 'Somehow our detective didn't pick up on that. You sound so unhappy though. Please tell me what's wrong...'

And Lucy compressed her lips, fighting the tears positively attracted by that soft, understanding sibling voice. 'I *can't* tell you—'

'You can tell me anything,' Polly assured her. 'Ellie and I are here and ready and willing to help you if you need us.'

'That's good to know but I still can't tell you,' Lucy repeated doggedly.

'Is your child's father abusive?' Polly demanded worriedly. 'Are you at risk in any way?'

'No...*no*!' Lucy insisted, hastening to shut down that suspicion. 'Look, I've just found out that my father blackmailed my bridegroom into marrying me! That's why I'm upset.'

'Right...' Polly's momentary hesitation spoke volumes and Lucy winced. 'But you're not responsible for what your father does. Lucy, you only have to say the word and, wherever you are and no matter what time of day it is, we'll have you picked up.'

'That's a very generous offer,' Lucy framed, deeply touched.

'Please think about coming to stay with us for a while...you'd be very welcome and it would give you a breathing space in which to decide what you want to do next,' her sister pointed out.

'I'll certainly think about it but I have to go now. I'm sorry. I'll phone you again when I have more time to talk.'

Lucy thrust her phone guiltily back into her bag, wondering what had possessed her to say so much to a woman she had never met. Now Polly probably thought she was more than a little weird. She headed down to the powder room on the ground floor to repair her make-up. Her mascara had run and she asked herself why she had been reduced to tears. The shock of Kreon's confession? The knowledge that Jax had only proposed to protect his cantankerous old father from the humiliation of having it known that his elder son had not been his? Whatever, it was her wedding day and she was on show and she had to get over her emotional reactions and behave normally.

'Where the hell have you been?' Jax demanded as he strode out of the function room to intercept her and closed his hands round her arms to hold her still. 'Is Bella OK?'

'She's fine. I was talking to someone,' Lucy told him, colliding with his stunning black-fringed green eyes and experiencing a jolt not unlike an electric shock.

Jax stared down at her. 'Have you been crying?' he asked, noticing the very faint hint of pink round her eyelids, which he was certain hadn't been visible earlier.

'No, for goodness' sake,' Lucy parried with an uneasy laugh. 'Why would I have been crying?'

Jax had no idea but he could see that Lucy's naturally sunny aura had dimmed. Perhaps Bella was playing up, he reasoned. Weddings were stressful and a strange place and a strange nanny could well have upset his daughter. He dropped a hand to Lucy's spine and guided her back into the function room and towards the top table.

The meal was served. It melted in Lucy's mouth but she might as well have been eating sawdust for all the pleasure it gave her. Her father-in-law asked her some very awkward questions about her past life and she answered as best she could, struggling to breeze lightly past her years in care and becoming much more animated when he asked about Bella.

A professional singer entertained them and then the dancing began. Jax had to almost drag Lucy onto the floor because she couldn't dance very well and was covered in blushes at the thought of having to perform in front of people.

'I just wish this day was over,' she confided, pushing her face against his chest, realising that he was so tall that, from one angle at least, she could literally hide herself.

'You and me both,' Jax admitted, wondering if his father had said something cutting to make her appear so subdued and feeling surprisingly angry at that suspicion.

Of course, the wedding he had been blackmailed into agreeing to could hardly be a source of pleasure for him, Lucy reckoned wretchedly. And what must he think of her father now? He probably knew Kreon had already spent a couple of years of his youth in a cell and now he would believe that Kreon belonged in prison and would think less of her because of it. People did judge you on your background and relatives. Not that he had ever thought that much of her to begin with, Lucy reminded herself unhappily, recalling how she had been cast off like an old shoe in Spain.

'In another few hours we'll be on our way,' Jax remarked, long brown fingers sliding down her back to gather her closer.

Heat curled between her thighs as she felt the evidence of his arousal. Her mouth ran dry. Evidently blackmail didn't douse Jax's libido. He still wanted her. Was that something to celebrate? Or something more to beat herself up about? Was she supposed to settle gratefully for being his sexual outlet? Was that all she was worth? All she deserved? She didn't know any longer. Her brain in turmoil, she forced herself to relax into the hard, muscular warmth of his hold and allowed him to slow-dance her round the floor. Other people were dancing now as well and she no longer felt like the centre of attention.

'Where will we be on our way to?' she asked belatedly.

'That's a surprise,' Jax admitted, still taken aback by what his father had done.

The little island of Tifnos was the Antonakos home but Jax had yet to even spend a night there. As a boy he had been ferried out there but only on day trips to attend several big family social occasions and as an adult he had flown to the island regularly to consult with Heracles about business. But it had never been *his* home because when he had been young he had been lucky if his father even acknowledged his presence among so many other guests. In truth he had always felt like an intruder and an outsider in his father's house and the startling concept of making Tifnos his base raised all sorts of conflicting feelings.

'Oh...' Lucy framed, drinking in the scent of him with flared nostrils. There was definitely something scientific in the effect of pheromones on attraction, she conceded ruefully. She loved Jax's smell; that indefinable combination of designer cologne and husky male had called to her from his first kiss.

Her eyes prickled again and she wrinkled her nose to hold the stupid tears back. Her husband, *blackmailed* into marrying her. Knowing that, she found it a challenge to believe that she could be a true bride and wife. In fact, Kreon's intervention and use of pressure made a nonsense of the entire day. She felt utterly humiliated. She wondered when she would work up the nerve to discuss what Kreon had done with Jax and how he would react when she did. He could well be furious that she had found out. His ferocious pride would rebel against her knowing that he could be forced into doing anything.

She was heading for the bridal suite to get changed for their departure when she saw Kat Valtinos walking towards her and suppressed a sigh because she wasn't in the mood to be patronised or bitched at over the head of Jax.

'Lucy...' Kat murmured with a bright artificial smile. 'Your big day's almost over.'

'Yes. We're leaving soon.' Lucy busied herself fishing out the card to open the door. Kreon and Iola had already taken Bella home for the night and her daughter would be staying with them for the first week Jax and Lucy were away.

'Well, enjoy it while you can,' Kat advised with saccharine sweetness. 'It's not as if your marriage will last long.'

As Lucy thrust the door open she simply ignored the brunette, refusing to be drawn into an exchange with her. Kat had hated her two years ago in Spain for attracting Jax and, from what she had seen of Jax and Kat in the newspapers, Kat must still have cherished hopes of something more coming from their long friendship.

'Jax will take the kid and dump you again,' Kat murmured lethally. 'Don't say you weren't warned.'

Lucy closed the door firmly behind her. Pale and shaky after that nasty little threat of what could be, she concentrated on removing her gown and freshening up. She pulled on a light dress and thrust her sore feet into sandals, touching up her make-up with a light hand. Kat was such a shrew, she reflected ruefully. Jax would *never* try to take Bella from her. Why would he do such a cruel thing? Or even think about separating a mother from her child? It wasn't as though she was an unfit mother. All right, she wasn't perfect. She had been known to snarl a little when Bella tried to get her out of bed at dawn but she *loved* her daughter. Nothing pleased Lucy more than the ability to give Bella all the little things she had never had herself, the small stuff like bedtime stories, favourite foods and lots of hugs.

Her luggage packed and then collected, Lucy went to meet Jax. A limo ferried them to the airport, where they boarded a helicopter.

'Are we going on the yacht?' she asked before the noise of the engine made any conversation impossible.

'No. Tifnos,' Jax told her simply.

And Lucy nodded, secretly intimidated by the prospect. She had read about the fabled private island Heracles had bought as a base in the eighties. Her father-in-law was reputed to live in feudal splendour there in a house that had never been photographed or shown in any publication. But it was supposed to have gardens that could rival the Garden of Eden, a private zoo and literally hundreds of staff.

Lucy felt inadequate. She was far too ordinary for such a backdrop. She had always been ordinary and had once thought that that was what attracted Jax to her. She didn't put on airs, she didn't say things she didn't believe to impress and when she didn't know something she admitted it. Unexpectedly, Jax closed a large hand over hers and then slowly laced his fingers with her own. His thumb massaged her inner wrist soothingly. It was as if she had hoisted a flag telegraphing panic and he had picked up on it. Or as if he was a little apprehensive too...

An idea she swiftly dismissed, for Tifnos was the Antonakos home and he had to be well accustomed to it.

It was fully dark by the time helicopter landed and Jax scooped her out onto the helipad. Momentarily she was thrilled by the dark heavens filled with thousands of the stars that were never visible in the city. Their luggage was piled into a beach buggy and Zenas took the wheel to drive them up a steep hill road hedged in by a forest of pine trees.

And then at the top the Antonakos house stretched like a giant illuminated cruise ship.

'It's big,' she said abruptly.

'Yep, for a man who doesn't like to entertain, Heracles built a very large house,' Jax conceded wryly.

They stepped into a foyer glossy and glittering with pristine marble and chandeliers. It looked exactly like a plush hotel reception without the desk. A double staircase swanned up to the next floor, each tread wide enough to march an army.

'Think movie set,' Jax urged. 'My mother redesigned the entrance, so there are some very theatrical touches.'

A small middle-aged Greek man approached them with a tray of welcoming drinks. Jax passed her a champagne flute but demurred on his account. 'I don't like champagne,' he admitted.

Lucy drank down hers to be polite while she peered into rooms furnished with the kind of opulence that just screamed old money to her. There were statues and collections and cabinets and elaborate artwork everywhere she looked. Suddenly she understood why there were supposedly hundreds of staff. It would take a fair number to look after so many possessions.

Jax set down her glass for her and closed his hand over hers and told the hovering manservant whom he addressed as Theo that they were going to bed.

'Wasn't that a little…offhand?' she pressed self-consciously as they climbed the stairs.

'It's one in the morning and it's our wedding night,' Jax intoned, his hand tightening on hers. 'We can get chatty tomorrow.'

She thought about what she had been avoiding thinking about and colour mantled her cheeks as Jax walked her into a vast room overflowing with urns of white roses and lilies, ornamented with trailing ivy. It was magnificent but not as magnificent as the vast divan bed on the dais scattered with rose petals.

'Heracles wasn't joking when he said he'd set the house up for the bridal couple,' Jax conceded with forbidding cool.

'It's beautiful,' Lucy muttered, because it was and she was grateful that her father-in-law had been prepared to make the effort on their behalf. 'But maybe a little too grand for the likes of me.'

'The "likes of me" now happens to be my wife,' Jax reminded her in reproof. 'And nothing is *too* grand or *too* good for my wife.'

'I'll get used to it…it's just a little overwhelming coming to a house like this,' Lucy confided.

'It's ours now,' Jax revealed, sharing his father's plans with her. 'I think he's hoping we'll go forth and multiply now for him.'

Lucy shrugged a slim shoulder, making no comment on that possibility.

'I think Bella's enough for us at present. I still have to learn how to be a father,' Jax completed, making his opinion clear. 'Do you want a drink or anything to eat? There're snacks waiting on the trolley.'

'No. I only want to get my shoes off,' Lucy admitted, dropping down into a luxurious armchair with a sigh. 'My feet are hurting.'

'Let me…' In the most disconcerting way, Jax crouched down lithely at her feet and unfastened her shoes to slip them off. 'You have such tiny feet. They used to fascinate me.'

Long brown fingers gently stroked the back of a delicate ankle and Lucy snatched in a sudden startled breath because her skin felt super sensitive, as though he had touched her somewhere much more intimate.

'All that got me through the day was the glorious

thought of sating myself inside you again, *koukla mou*,' Jax said huskily, rising to lift her bodily out of the chair and settle her down on the huge bed.

Eyes flying wide, cheeks flushing, Lucy stared up at him with bright blue eyes.

'So, why do you look like a cornered rabbit?' Jax asked pleasantly. 'You've been acting strangely all day.'

CHAPTER EIGHT

'I... I FELT OVERWHELMED,' Lucy told him and it was true.

The cathedral wedding, the sleek bejewelled Antonakos relatives and guests and the absence of any actual friends aside of her father's had weighed her down. The constant stares and the low buzz of conjecture hadn't helped either but when someone as rich as Jax married a waitress, who was the mother of his child, people stared and speculated. The wedding had been a strain and her father's confession of wrongdoing had crushed her. It had been the ultimate humiliation to learn that only Kreon's criminal act had made it possible for her to marry Jax.

And yet what could they possibly *do* about it now? Kreon had confessed too late to change anything. If she and Jax were to part this very night, it would cause a major scandal and she knew Jax wouldn't want to invite that media attention, which meant that at the very least they would have to stay married for a few months to make any breakup appear less worthy of comment.

'I can understand that,' Jax conceded, removing his jacket in a lazy fluid movement.

And Lucy watched him with a fast-beating heart, still wondering what she should do and how she should be behaving. Yet with a good ninety per cent of her being she craved the intimacy that being with Jax would give her. She wanted forgetfulness. She wanted to sink into the comfortable depths of the massive bed and shut the rest of the world out to take refuge in Jax. Even if he wasn't really hers and possibly wouldn't be hers for very long. His dazzling green eyes gleamed in the low-lit room, so bright against his dark bronzed skin, and her mouth ran dry.

Tugging his shirt from his waistband, he came back to the bed and sank down behind her to unzip her dress. She sat there like a little statue, her heart thudding like crazy in her chest as he lifted the garment up over her head, leaving her clad only in the white lace lingerie she had worn with her wedding gown. Sliding upright again, he unbuttoned his shirt, displaying a wide slice of his torso, well-defined muscles coming into view as he shed the shirt.

And she was as entranced by his sheer male beauty as she had once been in Spain, feasting her eyes on him with feminine appreciation. Jax worked out and it showed. He was all lean muscle and controlled power.

'Take the rest off,' he urged. 'I want to look at you.'

Her face burned as she reached behind her back to unclasp her bra. She had never done that before in front of him. Her clothes had once vanished beneath his skilled hands and she hadn't had to think about it or ever feel particularly naked. But there in that silent bedroom she was insanely aware of her body and its deficiencies as she let the bra fall. Most of the pregnancy weight had fallen away but there was no denying that she was curvier at bust and hip and there was an obvious scar low on her belly from the Caesarean she had had to have. Her waist was bigger too, she thought nervously, anxiously cataloguing every flaw. And this was a guy accustomed to the flawless female bodies of underwear models.

Jax studied the pouting swell of her pink-tipped breasts with intense pleasure, arousal flashing through him with storm-force potency. Everything about her daintiness appealed to him because her slender lines became lush in all the right highly feminine places. And he knew exactly what would happen when he touched her. He knew she would respond to him in a way no other woman ever had and that there would be nothing fake or exaggerated about it. Anticipation gave him the ultimate high.

'I'm not perfect,' she warned him tightly as her fingers flirted with the band of her knickers. 'Well, I never was, but—'

A flashing grin flared across Jax's lean, darkly

handsome features as he came down on one knee on the bed and yanked her playfully to him by her ankles. 'You're perfect for me... I only want to see you.'

Sharply disconcerted by that teasing assault, Lucy looked up at him with apprehensive eyes of blue. He hooked his hands into her knickers and dragged them off, lowering her back gently against the pillows and then rearranging her to his own satisfaction, her legs parted and her hands by her side.

'I'd love a painting of you looking like this, all spread out and waiting for me, but I couldn't stand the artist seeing you naked,' he admitted thickly, peeling off his trousers and his boxers in an impatient movement.

Lucy lay there feeling like a sacrifice and yet she was quite ridiculously excited by his scrutiny and the thrusting fullness of his arousal. He was so ready for her, was always ready. He made her feel as though her body were flawless and the desire he made no attempt to hide warmed the sore place inside her where her father's betrayal had contrived to undermine her self-esteem.

Jax joined her on the bed and went straight for her mouth with hungry, driving kisses that parted her lips and sent a current of high-voltage expectation flying through her trembling length. Her fingers clutched into his spiky, messy black hair and tears burned behind her lowered eyelids because she wanted him so much that she hurt with the wanting. It felt too intense, too desperate and that wasn't what she wanted to feel. She needed to stay in control, she told herself, remember what was real and what wasn't real. And what they had now *wasn't* real. Why did thinking that drive a knife through her when it was only the truth?

'I can't get enough of you,' Jax growled between the urgent biting kisses that bruised her lips and the devastating plunge of his tongue that made her slight body jackknife in reaction beneath his.

'We've got all night,' she whispered through rosy swollen lips, eyes glazed with passion.

'I've got a hunger that one night won't come anywhere near satisfying,' Jax told her rawly, fisting a hand in her tumbling curls as he snaked a string of kisses down over her collarbone and found a plump, pointed nipple to torment with attention.

'Oh… Jax,' she gasped, a fire trail of tingles lighting up from her breast to her pelvis where a warm damp sensation pulsed.

With difficulty Jax dragged his lips from her writhing body and stared down at her. She was his wife now. Signed, sealed and delivered. In the strangest way, he registered, he *liked* that, liked that ring on her finger that marked her as his and loved the way she was looking up at him as though he had hung the moon.

'You will be very tired tomorrow,' Jax forecast

without hesitation. 'I'm planning to take everything you can offer and then some more.'

Without hesitation, Lucy leant up and claimed his sensual, taunting mouth for herself, revelling in the instant rush of hungry need he betrayed. He scored the edge of his teeth across her full lower lip, dallied over the sensitive skin below her ear and then returned to his self-imposed worship of her full breasts. He lashed the hard little tips into swollen, throbbing sensitivity and her hips rose beneath his long, lean physique until he settled a leg between hers, giving her the pressure she craved at the crux of her body.

The demanding ache at the heart of her spread, sending little tingles through every skin cell, building and building her tension. He teased her nipples with his teeth and the heat of a climax simply exploded through Lucy in a glorious rush that made her cry out and jerk under him.

'That's one...' Jax husked with satisfaction.

'You're counting now?' Lucy mumbled distractedly, dragged into brain-dead lethargy by the shimmering backwash of sheer pleasure.

'I always was goal-orientated,' Jax reminded her, working his passage slowly down her quivering length.

Tell him you know about the blackmail, a guilty little inner voice urged her. But that would unleash a very difficult conversation after an extremely long and trying day. In any case Jax was reasonably happy at this precise moment, she decided, and she didn't want to spoil things. Later they would both be more relaxed and less tense. He tugged her thighs apart and buried his mouth there and suddenly her brain didn't have any space left in which to be rational. Suddenly she became a twisting, gasping creature at the mercy of her own sensual responses.

Jax slid a finger through her silky folds. He stroked her, smiling as she moaned and shifted, striving to urge him on, but in bed Jax was always in control, most particularly because Lucy had no control.

'Torture!' she muttered between gritted teeth, a rosy flush and perspiration slicking her skin as she thrashed under his ministrations, gasping as he hit the exact spot where she was most sensitive.

'I love the taste of you,' Jax growled, the vibrations of his dark deep drawl pulsing through her tender flesh.

Involuntarily, her body erupted again, driven to the point of explosive climax by the intensity of her excitement. She screamed his name and jerked and then fell still, wonder creeping over her that anyone could possibly wreak such havoc with her system and give her that much pleasure.

'*Thee mou*, I want you so much,' Jax ground out as he slid over her, his hands strong on her hips to angle her back.

He entered her slowly, urging her tender flesh to

open for him and stretch, and the sensation made her dizzy with yearning and wildly impatient for more. He eased back and then pushed in hard and deep and her body convulsed and tightened round him, intense sensation ravishing her. A string of tiny sounds was wrenched from her parted lips as he ground into her and picked up the pace, raw excitement flooding her as she tilted up to meet him, hot, damp and abandoned as the wild roller coaster of sensation raged on and on. He slammed into her with primal force and her body just splintered from the inside out, taking her apart in pieces so that she slumped back on the bed, barely aware of his muffled groan of completion but welcoming the warm, heavy weight of him.

Empty of all conscious thought, Lucy skated her hands over Jax's smooth damp back and then wrapped her arms round him tightly. He was struggling to catch his breath close to her ear and she smiled and twisted her head to kiss him on the cheek.

Jax froze as though she had crossed some invisible boundary line. He refused to do that stuff with her again. Bone and sinew he rejected any show of affection that came from her and he yanked back from her and rolled away. He wasn't buying into that again with her, no way! She had given him that same hugging and petting and apparent warmth in Spain and he knew it was meaningless. He had known that when he saw her in that alleyway having sex with another man. As that cringe-making memory returned, Jax wanted to smash a fist into the wall.

That was better left buried and he knew it, particularly now that they were married. When he thought about it, he felt seething anger and violent. Forgiveness wasn't in his vocabulary and forgetting wasn't in his nature. There wasn't any reason for him to think about that sordid episode, he told himself grimly. All he had to do for his own protection was remember that she was treacherous and watch out when she was around other men.

When Jax jerked away from her and headed for what she assumed was the bathroom, Lucy felt as if he had slapped her in the face. He had recoiled from her as if she were contagious, as if he couldn't *bear* her touch. After such intimacy, that hit hard and hurt, spelling out the message that once he had had sex, he was up and away, any pretence of courtesy or caring set aside and rejected.

She felt hollow and very, very foolish. This was the aggressive male her father had blackmailed into marrying her and this was the payoff, she assumed sickly. Evidently he had taken the only thing he actually wanted from her and now she was like an abandoned toy, a distraction good enough only to be tossed back in the cupboard until the next time he wanted to take her out and play with her.

'You don't like it when I touch you after sex,' she accused baldly.

Jax shot her a winging glance from narrowed green eyes that glittered. 'Because it's fake.'

Lucy sat up. 'It wasn't fake,' she told him but he had already vanished into the bathroom and within seconds she heard the sound of a shower running.

Well, Jax needn't think that was the end of the conversation just because he wanted it that way, Lucy thought angrily. She scrambled out of bed and grabbed up her handbag to extract the letter that Kreon had given her. Whether she liked it or not, it was time to be open and honest. She opened the bedroom door and found their luggage piled outside. She lifted a case and dragged it in, opening it up to remove a light cotton robe. Nothing slinky about her nightwear, she reflected ruefully. Iola had insisted on buying her some stuff and the prospect of Jax gazing in disbelief at her chain-store PJ's had persuaded her. She wrapped herself in the robe, watching out of the corner of her eye as Jax strode naked into what sounded like an en-suite dressing room because she could hear drawers being rammed open and shut and cupboard doors being slammed. My goodness, he was in a bad mood…so much for her assumption that intimacy would bring relaxation and a release of tension!

Jax reappeared, clad in a pair of faded jeans and a black tee shirt that clung to his muscular torso. He headed straight for the trolley and opened it before lifting a plate and piling food on it. 'Would you like anything?' he asked with studious politeness and she wanted to slap him for his tone.

'Not right now, thanks,' she murmured tightly. 'I have something for you... Kreon gave it to me today.'

Jax swung round, fully acknowledging her for the first time, his lean, darkly handsome face guarded until he saw and immediately recognised what was in her hand and he stalked forward to snatch it from her with a profound look of revulsion.

'Were you in it *with* him?' Jax shot at her accusingly, for most ironically that possibility hadn't occurred to him and right there and then he called himself an idiot for not having suspected her active involvement in Kreon's blackmail threat.

Lucy's chest swelled on a stark indrawn breath of shock as she drew herself up to her full unimpressive height. 'Are you certifiably insane?' she demanded in fiery rebuttal of that suspicion. 'Yesterday, *after* the wedding, Kreon told me what he had done to you because he felt guilty. He knew he'd done wrong—'

'*Diavolos...*' Jax derided. 'Kreon felt guilty? You will never know what a comfort that is to me!'

'He did wrong but he's not a bad man and the mistake you made was in not immediately coming to me about my father's threat and the existence of that letter,' Lucy condemned with conviction. 'I believe I could've stopped it because he would have been too ashamed to continue with it once I knew about what he was doing.'

'And pigs fly and there's two blue moons in the sky,' Jax scorned, shaking his tousled dark head in wonderment, green eyes as cutting as sword blades. 'I'll ask you one more time...were you aware of his intentions?'

'No, I blasted well wasn't!' Lucy shouted back at him, her blue eyes flooded with angry, defensive discomfiture. 'How can you even ask me that? I wasn't expecting you to ask me to marry you, wasn't even thinking along those lines!'

Jax cocked his proud dark head back, black curling lashes semi-screening his stunning eyes. 'It's done now.'

'Yes,' she acknowledged uncomfortably. 'But I had nothing to do with the blackmail or any idea of what was going on behind the scenes—'

'But it all worked in your favour, all the same,' Jax spelt out with contempt. 'You got to marry into the Antonakos family.'

'Well, from where I'm standing now, on my wedding night, marrying into the Antonakos family is not the triumph it's purported to be!' Lucy shot back at him furiously, an angry flush mantling her cheeks. 'In fact it feels like hell, most particularly when I seem to have a husband who can happily have sex with me and then virtually push me away afterwards!'

'I don't cuddle…*ever*,' Jax stressed.

'Bella needs cuddles so you'll have to revise your rule and I need them too,' Lucy flung back at him rawly. 'So, if you want sex, you'll do it.'

An unholy flare of rage lit up Jax's eyes, lightening them to the brilliance of sea glass gleaming in sunshine. 'I've put up with a hell of a lot but I won't stand for *that*!' he raked back at her, every word slicing through the air like a knife. 'I married you. Be grateful for it because you're getting nothing else from me but the name and the money and a father for your child!'

And as Lucy stood there staring at him, involuntarily unnerved by the sheer force of his rage, she stilled a shiver, appalled by that assurance. 'That's not enough for me,' she muttered shakily.

'Tough,' Jax enunciated with clarity. 'That's all you'll be getting now and in the future.'

With that final statement of punitive intent, Jax strode out of the room and just left her there. Lucy ate through a whole plate of profiteroles and drank coffee and then felt sick. Her whole world had fallen into pieces round her feet and, with it, any sense of security. She lurched into the bathroom where she was sick and when she felt strong enough to stand up again she went for a shower. She knew she would never look at a profiterole again. She would never look at Jax the same way again either for she had just seen a side of him that he had never shown her before.

Now she knew what she really *hadn't* wanted to know. He hadn't wanted to marry her. In fact he had absolutely hated and thoroughly resented having to marry her. He had suppressed that fury successfully throughout the day and she had provoked him into expressing it by asking for something more: a stupid cuddle, of all things. Her eyes stung and she looked heavenwards as she struggled to control her wildly see-sawing emotions. As far as Jax was concerned he had already given her more than enough: his famous name, his great wealth, his readiness to be a father. *Your* child, he had called Bella, not *our* child.

Why would he care that none of that would be sufficient to make her happy? Why would he care that she was hurting so bad that she wanted to scream with the pain of it? He hadn't asked her to care about him and she didn't know when or how she had started caring again. In Spain it had begun with a smile, a shared look of understanding and discussion, a touch of his hand, six weeks of breathless excitement and more happiness than she had ever experienced before she lost it all again.

But, Jax had reappeared in her life and somehow shreds of those old feelings had taken root again deep down inside her where she didn't explore very often. *She* cared. Much more than he deserved. But was that a true or fair view? Kreon had been vicious and

Jax had been strong-armed by family affection into making a sacrifice he didn't want to make. Sadly, Jax wasn't any keener on the concept of marriage than he had ever been.

So, what did that leave her to work with? Lucy blinked back tears and went to clean up her face again, dashing on a little make-up in a desperate hope of relocating a hint of a lingering bridal glow. Unhappily she looked tired and heavy-eyed and pale and even bronzer didn't help. In the end she washed it all off again before she went to look for Jax.

It was the early hours of the morning but everywhere was lit up. She didn't even know what she was going to say to him but she knew that she had to deal with the situation and make something out of the mess Kreon had created. After all, they had Bella to consider and while Lucy was prepared to let go of her own dreams she wasn't prepared to give up on her dream of giving her daughter a normal family life.

She peered into empty room after empty room on the ground floor and then she found him, sprawled with a glass in his hand on a huge fancy padded lounger sited on a wide terrace from which he was watching the sun come up in a glorious multicoloured reflective rainbow over the dark sea far below the house. She hesitated beside the patio doors and then noticed that the phone he was studying was displaying a wedding photo of their daughter. And that discovery softened her and empowered her in a way nothing else could have done into moving forward.

'Jax?' she murmured uncertainly.

'We have to make a go of it…or at least *try*…for her,' Jax breathed in a raw undertone without turning his head.

'Yes…' It was exactly what Lucy wanted to hear and yet she still felt as though her heart were breaking inside her because she knew that she wanted so much more from him.

'I'm drunk,' Jax confided gruffly, wishing he weren't, wishing he were better at handling his own emotional turmoil. 'But drowning your sorrows doesn't help. It only darkens everything more.'

In the tense silence, Lucy dropped down onto the smaller lounger beside his. She didn't recline, she sat on the side of it, rigid-backed and still. A photo lay on the table between them and she lifted it. It was a picture of another little girl, a little girl who looked similar enough to Bella to be her sister.

'Who's this?' she asked worriedly, immediately wondering if Jax had another child.

'My little sister, Tina. The reason why I didn't need to wait on DNA test results to know that Bella was mine,' Jax explained reluctantly.

'I didn't know you had a sister.'

'Hardly anyone knows. When she died it was hushed up,' he muttered.

Lucy frowned. 'Your father's child?'

'No. From my mother's second marriage to an actor. He was half her age. It fell apart quickly. By then Mariana was accidentally pregnant and as a devout Catholic there was no question of her not giving birth. Valentina was born the summer I was twelve. Mariana was determined to keep her a secret because she couldn't bear the idea that her adoring fans would pity her for being abandoned a second time with a child. Unfortunately, she could never keep household staff for long. I looked after the baby that summer—'

'At twelve years old?' Lucy gasped although she was trying hard not to react to what he was telling her. 'Where was your mother?'

'Zonked out of her skull on prescription drugs... the way she always was,' Jax confided grudgingly. 'I got attached to Tina. She was a sweet kid. Mariana got another nanny before I went back to boarding school and for a couple of years everything was fine. I saw Tina in the holidays. And then Mariana had a fight with the nanny the day before she held a pool party...and Tina drowned because nobody was looking after her. My mother was a legendary star and the studio ensured that the death and the burial were dealt with very discreetly.'

'I'm so sorry, Jax,' Lucy whispered shakily.

'The worst part of it was that nobody ever mentioned Tina again. It was like she'd *never* existed.'

Lucy slid to her feet and settled on the big lounger by his side, one arm draping over him protectively.

'I don't cuddle,' he told her argumentatively.

'You're not cuddling,' Lucy assured him. 'I'm cuddling you.'

'I really don't need *or* like that sort of stuff,' he growled.

'Of course you don't. You're just tolerating me to be polite.' Lucy sighed, feeling the rigid tension in his muscles ease and snuggling into the powerful heat of his long, lean frame. 'You have such good manners, Jax.'

'I *do*?' Jax said in surprise, flipping over to face her, green eyes clear as emeralds in the dawn light.

'Most of the time,' Lucy murmured with amusement, colliding with those gorgeous eyes of his, eyes full of so much hunger and uncharacteristic uncertainty. 'I *wasn't* part of the blackmail plan.'

'I know...' Jax rubbed his dark stubbled jaw against her shoulder as if in apology. 'But I think I preferred you not knowing about what your father did.'

'I would've preferred that too,' Lucy admitted. 'But it happened and we have to deal with it.'

Assertive hands tugged at the edges of her robe and the sash before sliding beneath the crisp fabric. 'Naked,' Jax savoured. 'I like, *glyka mou*.'

Lucy bridled. 'I wasn't thinking about that when I came looking for you. I couldn't be bothered poking through another case to find clothes...'

'Shush...' Jax murmured, long brown fingers rubbing with devastating expertise over the most sensitive spot on her entire body to set off a devastating tingling awareness before sliding down below. 'I want you.'

'Here?' she gasped in consternation even as her slender thighs parted and her hips shifted in a rhythm as old as time.

'I sent the staff to bed when we arrived. Poor Theo had kept them all up,' Jax told her. 'I don't need attention twenty-four-seven…except from you.'

Lucy's rosy lips parted on a helpless gasp. 'Twenty-four-seven?' she framed with difficulty.

'I'll make it well worth your while,' Jax promised, crushing her ripe mouth urgently under his as he unzipped his jeans and shifted over her with urgent intent. 'Let's take this back into honeymoon territory…'

And Lucy, at that moment malleable as clay in his expert hands with her body rising and burning and already defencelessly eager, had no objection to that plan. They had weathered the first storm, learned that for both of them Bella was their main focus. That had to be enough, she told herself urgently, a strangled sound escaping her convulsing throat as he pinned her under him and plunged into her with raw, hungry energy.

Pushing for more would only strain their relationship, which meant that *she* had to learn to settle for what she could get. And if that meant forgiving his suspicion that she could have been involved in her father's blackmail, she had to do it. It was early days, she reminded herself.

Yet how could he suspect her of such dishonest behaviour? And why did he assume that her affection was faked? Was his past so littered with unscrupulous lovers that trust was impossible for him?

CHAPTER NINE

'YOU WERE TELLING me about your adoptive parents,'
Jax reminded her as they walked along the deserted
beach three weeks later, walking Bella between them
to keep the little girl steady.

'Was I? They were good people. I was nine years
old and very fortunate to get a home at that age,'
Lucy declared wryly.

'I imagine you were a very pretty little girl. I'm
sure that helped.'

Lucy shrugged, thinking back to that brief three-
year period when she had been part of a family.
'They were very academic. When they took me on
they were warned that I'd fallen behind at school
and straight off they decided to hire tutors for me
in every subject.'

Jax frowned. 'Impatient, were they?'

'No, they were trying to help but it put me under
a lot of pressure. I was trying very hard to be everything they wanted and then I failed an important

exam, which meant I couldn't get into the school they had set their hearts on and they were really disappointed. I don't think I was the right child for them,' she admitted ruefully. 'But when they died in the car crash, all that ended and I went back into care because none of their relatives saw me as being part of the family. At the end of the day and whether you agree with it or not, blood counts.'

'Yes, doesn't it?' Jax agreed, thinking of his late brother, Argo, a good-natured, indolent young man, who with hindsight had been remarkably dissimilar to Heracles and Jax in nature.

Bella tugged her hand free of her mother's and pulled at Jax's jeans to be lifted. He hoisted her high and she giggled and rested her curly head down sleepily on his bare shoulder. Their interaction was so relaxed and natural now, Lucy thought with satisfaction, that it was hard to believe they had only met a month ago.

She and Jax hadn't lasted a whole week on the island without Bella. Lucy had never been separated from her daughter before and had decided a week was unnecessarily long when there was a nanny on the household staff, willing and able to give the honeymooners a break from childcare: Heracles had prepared for every eventuality when he entertained. But the rumour of a private zoo had proved to be just that—a rumour.

The gardens, however, were spectacular although

Jax and Lucy had spent more time on the beach, crunching through the pale sand to the water's edge where Lucy, who could not swim, liked to paddle. Never having enjoyed many such opportunities, she was not keen on trusting her body to either a swimming pool or the sea, but Jax had insisted that her learning to swim was a safety issue more than anything else. So, Lucy had braved swimming lessons with Jax, which they had both found equally trying, Jax because he was naturally impatient and Lucy because she was nervous.

Over the past three weeks they had learned so much about each other, she acknowledged cheerfully. Jax was a morning person, Lucy was a night person. They had spent a wonderful ten days cruising round the Mediterranean on his father's yacht, *Sea Queen*, docking at different islands to see the sights, dine out and shop. She loved to dance and they had enjoyed several really late nights out at clubs. He had bought her loads of clothes in hip boutiques on Crete and Mykonos and he had had a jeweller flown out to Tifnos for her to choose what he deemed to be the basics. A gold watch now encircled a wrist and gold hoops ornamented her ears. She had a diamond pendant, bracelet and earrings as well, which he had referred to as a 'belated' wedding gift. And Bella had a nursery overflowing with toys and clothing and picture books to go with the designer furnishings.

In fact, Lucy believed she already had almost everything she had ever wanted or ever dreamt of having. Jax had spoiled them both. He was marvellous with Bella, far more patient with her than he was with anyone else. He was making a huge effort to be a dad and she appreciated that when so many of his friends, smooth sophisticates whom they had met in the clubs where he was well known, had yet to even settle down. For a man who had never wanted to marry, Jax was settling down into family life remarkably well, she reflected gratefully.

Yet she couldn't forget that Jax was the same guy who had dumped her for 'boring' him two years earlier, the same guy who had seemed perfectly content with her one day and who had then cut her out of his life only days later. That past still made her insecure because she had no faith that she could accurately read Jax and estimate his state of mind with regard to her and their marriage. Of course, he seemed to do and say all the right things, but then he had done that before in Spain and look how that had ended!

'I'm hungry...' Jax curved a hand to Lucy's shoulder and steered her up the beach towards the buggy that would waft them up the steep hill. 'And I think our daughter needs a nap...and maybe I need one too, *glyka mou.*'

Lucy coloured. Heat licked at her feminine core as Jax sent her a glittering green glance of sensual enquiry. Dampness gathered between her legs, anticipation rising because that side of their relationship was outrageously healthy. He still wasn't doing the cuddling thing the way she wanted. No, with Jax what might start out as a cuddle invariably turned into sex. He said he couldn't be that close to her and touch her without wanting to get naked and energetic. There was nowhere they hadn't made love. They had indulged on the beach, in the pool, in the pine forest, in the labyrinthine privacy of the lush gardens, but most often in the delicious comfort of their own bed. The simmering flare-ups of passion that wound through their days felt so natural to her. It was as if Jax couldn't get enough of her, a thought she kept tactfully to herself, and that made her feel safer. She couldn't help viewing sex as a barometer to gauge the health of their marriage because Jax certainly wasn't any keener to discuss such things than he had ever been.

'It's those freckles. I can't resist them,' Jax said huskily, skimming the bridge of her nose with a teasing finger.

Lucy laughed because she hated her freckles, seeing them as imperfections, but Jax thought they looked delightfully natural, which of course they were. Did anyone draw in freckles? She thought not and smiled as they piled into the buggy. A pang of sadness infiltrated her mood because the honeymoon as such was almost over. Jax was meeting with Heracles about some big project in Athens the following morning and she was accompanying him because she planned to take Bella to visit her father and Iola. She was hoping that the passage of time since her wedding day and Bella's noisy presence would make the occasion less tense and awkward.

In actuality, Jax wasn't looking forward to the next day either. He intended to confront his father with the file Heracles had had sent to him on Lucy two years before. From what he had so far managed to establish the file was full of inaccuracies and outright lies and he needed to know if those lies had been a deliberate attempt to break up their relationship or the simple product of a lazy investigator and a case of mistaken identity. He could scarcely censure Kreon's ethics if his own father was guilty of the same lack of moral scruple when it came to getting the result he wanted most.

Even so, he still could not have said which answer he wanted to hear from Heracles because if the older man actually *believed* the contents of that file, it outraged Jax in a way he could not rationally explain. Yet he, more than anyone, knew Lucy was far from perfect. His mind skipped superfast over that acknowledgement and tucked the memory of that alleyway encounter back into the box where he kept it locked away. She had made an unforgivable mistake and he *had* to live with that…for Bella's sake, he told himself urgently, *only* for Bella's sake.

Bella's nanny took the little girl off to bed. Lucy went for a shower because she was hot and sandy and she wasn't at all surprised when Jax stepped into the shower with her, all lithe, wet bronzed skin and rippling muscles. She ran her hands up appreciatively over his torso and as the water jets shot at them, sprinkling even their faces with droplets, his mouth came crashing passionately down on hers. He tasted her with raw driving need and as always the strength of his hunger for her disconcerted her. He gathered her slippery body up and pinned her against the cold tiles, lifting her thighs round his waist while rocking and grinding against the tender triangle of flesh at the heart of her.

That fast she wanted him intolerably and with every probing plunge of his tongue she wanted him more. Evocative little noises were wrenched from low in her throat as skilled fingers teased and played to prepare her for his entrance. And then he tilted her back and thrust into her with vigour while she clung to his shoulders, her ankles wrapped round him. He grunted with raw male satisfaction, his hand supporting her hips as he pounded her yielding body with delicious force. Excitement writhed through Lucy in an unstoppable surge and she reached her peak with an involuntary cry, convulsive waves of exquisite pleasure rippling through her lower body as an orgasmic flush spread over her sun-dappled skin.

'I didn't use a condom,' Jax groaned in her ear as he slowly lowered her back to her own feet. 'Is that likely to be a problem?'

'Hopefully not,' Lucy muttered after doing some quick calculations and without looking directly at him as she stepped out of the shower and grabbed a towel. 'It's the wrong time of the month.'

What had he meant by that question? Was he asking her if she was willing to get pregnant again? Or was he worrying that she *would* conceive? And for that matter, was she willing to take that risk? Lucy thought not. She had not had an easy pregnancy the first time around and was not in a hurry to do it again, particularly when she did not yet feel secure with Jax. Even so, if she did conceive she would still welcome and love her baby.

But then what would it take for her to feel truly secure with Jax? she asked herself. Perhaps she was her own worst enemy and had quite unrealistic expectations of a marriage in which only one of them loved. She might not like the reality but their relationship was bound to be unbalanced with one of them wanting and hoping for more than the other.

'Did you know that the contents of that file were a complete fiction?'

'What do you want me to tell you?' Heracles slapped the file on Lucy back onto his desk and sighed heavily. 'I will not lie. I did what I felt I *had* to do.'

Sharply disconcerted, Jax tensed even more, anger roaring through his tall, powerful frame because he had somehow expected the older man to try and evade his very direct question. 'Why did you think you *had* to do anything? Why did you even think that it was your place to interfere? It wasn't as though I was talking about marrying her—'

'Jax…in the space of two weeks, you flew back to Spain *five* times to see her,' Heracles traded defiantly. 'That was enough for me to view her as a serious contender for something and when I discovered that she was the daughter of Kreon Thiarkis, well, to be really blunt…that was that. Thiarkis is a slippery customer, always has been, always will be and I will not apologise for not wanting a criminal's daughter involved with my family.'

'I know Kreon's history,' Jax interposed harshly. 'I know what he is and I can understand your concern but I was twenty-six years old, *not* a teenager, and you had no right to interfere.'

The older man stood his ground. 'I know I had no right but I didn't care. Years ago I watched Thiarkis charm my deluded first wife into paying for his legal representation in court when he was charged with fraud—'

'Two years ago, Lucy hadn't even *met* her father,' Jax pointed out rawly. 'What I had with her was our business alone, nothing to do with your ongoing distaste for Thiarkis. And far be it from me to say a word in Kreon's defence but for over thirty years he held onto a letter that would have made his fortune had he sold it to the press...'

Jax settled the letter Lucy had given him down on the desk. 'Your first wife confessed her sins on paper during her last days.'

His father turned grey before his eyes and dropped down suddenly into his office chair, studying the letter as if it were a cobra likely to strike out at him. 'Sofia was never discreet,' he muttered heavily. 'Are you telling me I have to thank Thiarkis for his restraint?'

'No,' Jax breathed in a driven undertone, having decided not to reveal the secret of Kreon's blackmail. 'But it's time you came to terms with the fact that he is Lucy's father and stopped visiting your experiences and your resentments on *my* life. I'm not Argo—'

'I know you're not,' Heracles acknowledged grimly. 'Argo always did as he was told and you *won't*, which is why I went behind your back in the first place. I assumed she would be wrong for you.'

'She's not,' Jax bit out curtly. 'But because of that file I treated her badly and now I have to tell her why.'

Heracles compressed his lips in disapproval. '*Do* you? I don't think that's a good idea. A wise man shares nothing with his wife but a bed.'

'Three wives and you *still* don't know better?' Jax derided with seething bite. 'Well, I do know better and I will not tolerate your meddling in my life. If you ever do anything like this again, I'm *out*.'

'You can't mean that,' Heracles breathed in consternation.

'I do. Blood counts but family counts more and you were out of my life for too many years to be considered family in the same way that I consider my wife and my daughter. They come first...*always*.'

Simmering with angry frustration, Jax sat in his limo in the heavy Athens traffic mulling over that confrontation. Heracles had finally apologised and at least his father had at last told him the truth. Jax hated secrets. He had grown up in an atmosphere of secrecy, continually urged never to tell anyone that his mother was 'ill', pregnant or involved with a man. As a boy, he had reacted to those warnings by deciding to never tell anyone at school that the famous Spanish movie star was his mother. It had been a rather pathetic ploy considering that the name Antonakos was too well known and just about everyone who was anyone knew his father had divorced Mariana for having an affair with one of her co-stars. But the practice of keeping his thoughts and feelings and personal details strictly private had been taught to him when he was very young and had become a habit he couldn't shake...until he'd met Lucy and told her things he had never told anyone before.

And if he was honest that experience had totally

unnerved him two years earlier. He had seen that he was veering into dangerous territory and had feared getting too involved with a woman again. *Feared?* No, obviously he had been in no hurry to admit that to himself. His mother had been frighteningly volatile, constantly ranging between high and low moods while using drugs as a crutch to get her through the day. Freed by Mariana's death from the powerful conviction that it was *his* responsibility to look after her, Jax had decided that emotion was a weakness and that a sensible man steered clear of it. Most of the time that had worked very well for him.

Until he'd met Lucy…

Until he'd met Bella…

Jax poured himself a stiff drink and drank it down. He *had* to tell Lucy. How could he *not* tell her? He reminded himself that she had married him even after what he had done in Spain. He reminded himself that she seemed happy. He didn't have to love her to make her happy. Hadn't he already proved that? Together they had the fathers from hell. Not her fault, not his fault either. He would give her the facts. She would be angry and hurt but she would forgive him. Jax knew he wasn't the forgiving type but he was convinced from recent experience that Lucy *was*. They had signed up to be a family for Bella's benefit. And that would be Lucy's bottom line because more than anything else, Jax reminded himself doggedly, after a life of turmoil Lucy craved security.

And he offered security, he offered a *lot* of security, he reflected with growing assurance. But it still really bothered him that she wasn't clingier and more open with him. The Lucy he remembered in Spain had been distinctly needy and clingy and, although he ran a mile from that trait in other women, for some reason he had liked that attribute in Lucy as much as he had liked her once flaky tell-all chatter. He had liked it when he was the first person she looked for in a room, when he was the only one she really smiled at or noticed, when she wrapped herself round him all night as though she was afraid he might attempt an escape. He had liked being told that he was loved even if in the end it had all turned out to be a lie.

But she didn't do those things any more even though he wanted her to. She was wary. Of course she was, he conceded, struggling to be fair, so, putting the truth out there was a sensible move, he told himself squarely. He would tell her what had really happened and she would forgive him because that was what Lucy did. And what choice would she have? a more cynical voice enquired. After all, she had betrayed his trust too...

'He's treating you well?' Kreon prompted while Iola was playing in the garden with Bella.

'Yes,' Lucy told her father flatly. 'But I won't discuss Jax with you.'

'A wife should be loyal to her husband,' Kreon remarked equably. 'I simply wanted you to be happy—'

'I can only be happy with a man who is happy to *be* with me,' Lucy countered drily, resisting the urge to remind him that he hadn't thought of that angle.

But with Jax being the very practical but reserved male that he was, he was more likely to make the best of a bad job than try to wriggle out of the commitment, particularly when his daughter was involved. Lucy showered and changed while telling herself that she had absolutely nothing to complain about. Whatever else, she was married to the love of her life. There was nothing she could do about the fact that she had only gained a wedding ring through her father's dirty tricks. But she knew that somewhere in the back of Jax's astute brain he would probably *always* associate her with her father's treachery and would never quite forgive her for his lack of choice and loss of freedom.

'He gave in to me very easily. That is *not* an Antonakos trait,' Kreon argued.

'Obviously he cares about his father.'

'I believe he cares more about you.'

Unconvinced by that startling claim, Lucy returned to the city villa with nerves run ragged by the strain of pretending for Iola's benefit that everything was fine between her father and her. She had been surprised that Jax hadn't objected to her visiting Kreon and Iola and then relieved because her father was still her father even though he was imperfect. *Imperfect?* Manipulative, sneaky, quick to jump on a golden opportunity even if it entailed blackmail, Lucy's brain added unhappily. But until she had met her father and learned about the existence of her sisters, she had believed that her father was her only living relative and his support and acceptance had meant a great deal to her. That he was capable of going to such lengths to secure a very rich husband for her still devastated her because of course it had to make a difference to her marriage and the light in which Jax saw her.

If Kreon hadn't interfered, who knew what might have happened? All right, they would clearly not have got married, she allowed ruefully, but at least Jax wouldn't have felt forced into doing something he didn't want to do.

Lucy had only just finished drying her hair when Jax strode into the bedroom. He paused for a second, appreciating the sight of her small slender figure in a summery blue dress, tumbling ringlets framing her piquant face. 'You look ridiculously pretty,' he heard himself say stiltedly, and he almost winced at that ill-timed opener because he had come upstairs to give her the investigation file.

Lucy angled her head to one side and gave him a questioning look. 'You never pay me compliments. What's wrong?'

He had called her pretty, not beautiful, and she

was more than happy with that, well aware that her looks weren't on the beauty level. In marrying Jax, she had boxed above her weight because *he* was the beautiful one in their relationship, standing there in his exquisitely tailored silver-grey suit, his stunning bone structure accentuated by a shadow of black stubble, gorgeous green eyes glittering like stars in his lean bronzed face.

'Never?' Jax was taken aback by her claim, only belatedly recognising that she was right. He thought such things but he very rarely voiced them out loud. 'I have something for you to read.'

He looked so very serious that Lucy's heart gave a sudden lurch inside her chest. 'OK,' she said apprehensively.

He extended the file. 'My father sent this to me two years ago in Spain. It's why I didn't turn up that last night.'

Lucy grasped the slim file and sank down heavily on the foot of the bed. 'Your father?' she queried with a bemused frown.

'He had discovered who your father was and apparently he was determined to break us up,' Jax explained flatly. 'The file is filled with what I now know to be lies about you.'

Lucy lowered her shaken gaze to the file, thoroughly off balanced by what he was revealing because it was coming at her out of nowhere. Suddenly he was talking about what had happened in Spain and admitting that he hadn't ditched her simply because he had got bored. 'You *now* know…?' she questioned with an uncertain questioning glance.

'I had my own investigation carried out,' he admitted smoothly.

And Lucy was even more shaken at the enormous amount of stuff that Jax had been hiding from her, not to mention the lowering reality of just how much his father had not wanted her in his family. She swallowed hard and, breathing in bracingly, she opened the file and straight away she could not credit what she was reading. It was a seriously exaggerated character assassination in print, from the outrageous allegation that she had convictions for drug dealing and soliciting sex to the fact that her age was quoted as being twenty-five.

'But how could you possibly have believed *any* of this?' she heard herself whisper with incredulous emphasis.

'It was in the early stages of my new relationship with my father and I trusted him. I had no reason to be suspicious of his motives because I had no knowledge of his acquaintance with your father or his dislike of him,' he pointed out flatly.

Lucy shook her head very slowly, an almost dazed light in her luminous blue eyes as she focussed on him. 'You misunderstood my question. I'm not asking why you believed your father but how on earth you could believe that kind of nonsense about *me*?

Soliciting *sex*? I was a virgin when we met!' she reminded him with sudden resentful heat. 'And you knew that!'

Jax compressed his lips, wearing the aspect of a male who would have liked to be anywhere but where he was at that moment. He shifted his feet uneasily. 'A woman can fool a man over stuff like that. She can pretend,' he began uncomfortably.

'Then you must have assumed my acting ability rivalled your mother's!' Lucy slotted in a little shakily because anger was rising now to cut through the shock of what she was learning. 'I just don't know what to say about all this…*stuff*!' she selected jaggedly, tossing the file down on the floor in disgust. 'I thought you *knew* me—'

'I thought I knew you too until I read that file,' Jax admitted curtly. 'But I had no good reason then to suspect my father of setting me up.'

'So, you're telling me then that he was responsible for me losing my job?'

'I didn't go into that with him… I was far too angry,' Jax confessed. 'But it's probable that he *was* responsible for that and for the manner in which you were treated as you were put off the yacht. If I had stayed long enough to get into that kind of detail I probably would have *hit* him…'

'Oh…' Lucy was a long way from forgiving him for having had so little faith in her but she was certainly mollified by that little speech.

'You were pregnant,' Jax pointed out, still stuck on that offence with an anger she could see making his lean, darkly handsome features rigid. 'You could have been seriously hurt. He could have killed his own grandchild…we could have lost Bella!'

Lucy warmed up to him a little more in response to that additional really quite emotional exclamation. Jax had only known her for six weeks in Spain. Six weeks and a handful of dates. They had finally become intimate during the final two weeks of that time frame. Why would he have distrusted his father? The father then riding high on the wave of finally deciding to accept and welcome the younger son he had once ignored?

Lucy felt that she had to be fair to Jax. After all, she had not distrusted Kreon when she first came to Greece, had she? It occurred to her that Jax was probably feeling much as she had felt on their wedding day, angry and hurt and defensive while wondering how someone he cared about and respected could have done such a thing to him.

'I think the very least you could have done was speak to me about the file and give me the chance to answer those allegations,' Lucy told him firmly. 'There is no excuse whatsoever for you failing to tell me about that file two years ago.'

And Jax's long, lean, powerful physique went rigid, shoulders squaring, legs straightening. 'Actually there is…'

'No, there's not.' Lucy could understand and forgive a great deal but he could not justify his complete failure to tell her what was going on either in the past or the present. 'You didn't even send me a text in Spain to tell me we were finished, for goodness' sake!' she exclaimed.

'I had my reasons,' Jax breathed in a raw undertone, his eyes gleaming like polished gems.

'Unacceptable reasons.' Lucy refused to give way. She often gave in to Jax because he had a very forceful personality but she knew she couldn't go through life without disagreeing with him occasionally. 'You owed me an explanation of some kind—'

'I owed you *nothing*!' Jax shot at her with sudden derision. 'I did come to see you the night after I received that file.'

Her brow had furrowed because she was beginning to feel a little lost in the dialogue, as though she had misinterpreted some crucial sentence. 'You *didn't* come to see me—'

'And do you know why?' Jax's hands knotted into fists because he felt like a volcano about to spew lava and somewhere in the back of his mind lurked a tiny voice asking him if he *really* wanted to say what he was about to say. But Jax didn't back down, had never learned *how* to back down. He only knew how to come out of a corner fighting and how to win. He had had a hell of a day and it wasn't getting better the way it was supposed to, it was only getting *worse* and that thought did nothing to cool his temper. He had done nothing wrong with Lucy, he was, in his own opinion, the injured party. He was not a vengeful man but he would not be accused of something he wasn't responsible for.

'If I did, I wouldn't be arguing with you or trying to get you to see my point of view,' Lucy parried.

'I bet you don't even remember that night...'

'I remember it very well,' Lucy admitted, lifting her chin. 'What's this all about, Jax? I'm getting confused—'

His eyes narrowed, his mouth flattening. 'I drove over to the bar and before I could get out of my car, I saw you walking down the alleyway in your red dress—'

'It wasn't me you saw,' Lucy sliced in thinly. When Jax had failed to turn up to see her the night before Lucy had stayed in her attic room after doing her shift, frantically hoping that Jax would magically appear with an explanation. Like a child waiting for Santa Claus she had refused to believe he wouldn't show up eventually and she had been terrified of somehow missing him. She had had that much faith in him, that much *trust*...

'It was you. You were with a man—'

'You're mistaken,' Lucy told him confidently.

'I followed you because I assumed you were heading for the entrance that led up to your room but you weren't,' Jax informed her stonily. 'You stayed outside to have sex with the man you were with against the wall.'

Her lashes fluttered up on disbelieving bright blue eyes and she stared back at him. 'You think that I had sex with some guy in the alley?' she demanded with a revulsion she couldn't hide. 'Are you kidding me?'

Lean, strong face shuttered and forbidding, Jax stood his ground because naturally he hadn't expected her to own up to her behaviour. 'You know I'm not kidding and what I saw that night is why you never heard from me again. There was no point in showing you that file when you were already with another man,' he proclaimed harshly. 'I don't need to apologise or make excuses for not approaching you again.'

'I agree,' Lucy said with wooden diction, shattered inside herself but holding it all together out of pride. 'If I had been with another man that soon, you owed me nothing. Clearly, it suited you very well to assume that night that the girl in the alley was me—'

'And what's that supposed to mean?' Jax shot at her suspiciously.

'Well, you'd seen that file and learned that your precious father did not approve of me. It was really incredibly convenient for you that in spite of everything you knew about me you decided to accept that file and *assume* that I was the sort of young woman who would have sex in an alley.'

Lucy could feel her cheekbones ache with the

strain of keeping her face composed but there was a much deeper ache of pain inside her chest. She knew he didn't love her. She knew he had never loved her. That wounding knowledge had chipped away at her upbeat outlook on their marriage and she had fought it off, telling herself to settle sensibly for what she could get. But for the first time ever, Lucy decided that Jax was *bad* for her.

Never mind the Antonakos fame, the money and the gorgeous looks. Two years back, she had told Jax that she loved him and she *had*, but he had given nothing back, not the words nor any other form of commitment. He had held back from her, he had always held back from her and now she finally knew why. But she deserved better. She deserved a man who would, at the very least, refuse to *believe* that she would have sex in public with some chance-met stranger. And Jax hadn't had that faith in her and probably never would have. A horrible sense of emptiness spread inside her. *Her* loving him wasn't enough.

'It *was* you. I recognised the dress,' Jax bit out, exasperated by the stretching silence and the strange way she was staring at him.

'Yes…you may have done but it wasn't me *wearing* the dress,' Lucy countered tightly. 'I loaned it to Tara that night because she had a hot date and I imagine she was fooling around in the alley because she could hardly bring a man back to the room we shared when I was there. Not everyone has a private room or a yacht available for these things...'

Jax froze. 'It *couldn't* have been her! Why would she have been wearing the dress I bought you?'

Lucy sent him a weary glance of exasperation. 'Because we shared our clothes. We didn't have much but what we had, we *shared*. Half the clothes you saw me wear that summer belonged to Tara.'

'It couldn't have been her,' Jax repeated again doggedly, struggling to remember her friend before dimly recalling the much more worldly blonde whom Lucy had worked and lived with.

Lucy shrugged a shoulder in a jerky movement. 'Well, it doesn't much matter after this length of time, does it?' she traded.

'It matters to me. And it *must* matter to you,' Jax told her with assurance.

'No, it doesn't,' Lucy responded heavily.

Jax hovered and clenched his teeth hard. He wanted it dealt with and then never mentioned again. But could it have been Tara in that stupid dress? It had been dark and Tara had had long blonde hair too. Between the street lights and the shadows, it was possible that he had been mistaken. And if he had been mistaken, it would be the very first time in Jax's life that he would ever be *grateful* to have made a mistake. Didn't she appreciate that? Didn't she understand what believing she would behave that way had done to *him*? Refusing to look at him, Lucy was staring at the tiled floor instead as if she were expecting it to start showing a movie and frustration racked Jax's tall powerful frame. *Women!* She had gone into a weird mood now and he would probably get nothing more out of her.

'I have a meeting. I was planning to reschedule it and take us back to Tifnos—'

'No, go to your meeting,' Lucy urged, her throat convulsing, and she still wouldn't let herself look at him because she didn't want what she felt in her heart to show.

'We can fly back in the morning,' Jax commented. 'The timing would probably suit Bella better than a late flight.'

Lucy listened to the door close on his exit and continued to sit there with tears rolling silently down her cheeks. Jax had just shown her how he really thought of her and how he saw her and it was…it *was* ugly, uglier than she could bear or forgive or comprehend. To think that all those weeks on the island he had believed that she had been unfaithful to him and yet he hadn't said a word, hadn't even given her the chance to explain or defend herself. It was so cruel, so unfair but you couldn't change a man, couldn't alter what went on inside his head.

Jax didn't trust her, had never trusted even a word she'd said. He had been her one and only lover and he couldn't even believe that. She had been too young and immature at nineteen to recognise how cynical and distrustful Jax was. She had realised that he was pretty jealous and possessive but her awareness had gone no deeper than that. She thought of him seeing Tara in that grubby alley and believing it was her and a stifled sob of pain and regret and humiliation was wrenched from her. That hurt so much and it seemed with Jax at that moment that he did nothing but hurt and disillusion her. She didn't want to stay married to a man like that, she *couldn't* stay married to a man who thought so little of her…

And when the wave of conflicting emotions began to tear at Lucy more than she could stand she dug out her phone and rang her sister, Polly, desperately needing a shoulder to cry on.

Polly was a terrific listener. Lucy let the whole sorry story of her relationship with Jax and Kreon spill out and, very satisfyingly, Polly was even more appalled by the alleyway accusation than Lucy had been.

'Come and stay with us, Lucy,' Polly suggested warmly. 'You need a holiday. I know you felt that you were happy with him at first but Jax doesn't seem to appreciate you the way a husband should. It's possible that he resents you for what your father did.'

To Lucy in that instant the prospect of walking away into a different environment shone like a bright welcoming light. 'I don't even know where you live, Polly,' she pointed out unevenly.

'In a country called Dharia. It's one of the Gulf States,' Polly explained.

Lucy was flummoxed by that news. 'I don't know how I'd get there or even how I'd get away from here.'

'Don't you worry about that,' Polly told her assertively. 'I will arrange everything. If you leave tonight, we'll be having breakfast together in the morning and I can get hold of Ellie and she could be here by this weekend. We really do want to meet you and your daughter, Lucy.'

'Leave…*tonight*?' Lucy gasped in astonishment, wondering if it would be wrong of her to take her daughter with her as well and then deciding that, just at that moment, losing both of them was what Jax deserved for his distrust.

'I don't think you should waste any more time on the Antonakos family. They don't love or value you but we *will*.'

And Polly's enthusiasm was the deciding factor for Lucy, who usually took more time to decide anything of a serious nature. But at least she didn't feel like crying any longer, she registered with relief, because crying after Jax had gone over her like a steam roller with his nasty allegations seemed feeble. Jax didn't want her and his father didn't want her in his precious family and her own father had seriously disappointed her. A fresh start and the friendship of her sisters looked a lot more promising than her current situation.

'Tonight will be fine,' she assured Polly. 'I'll start packing. I suppose it will be very hot?'

'Yes, but the pal—er...my place is air-conditioned,' her sister informed her.

CHAPTER TEN

JAX WAS STUNNED. He ran through the empty wardrobes again as if he expected to find Lucy curled up below the empty coat hangers in hiding. He wandered back to the empty nursery, stared into the even emptier cot and then hurriedly strode back downstairs again.

'Take me through it again,' he urged Zenas jerkily, struggling to master the kind of emotions he generally never allowed to see the light of day. Emotions like panic, fear and insecurity that could tear a man to pieces as they had once torn apart the boy he had been. Having frequently lived those emotions in childhood and adolescence, he had sworn never to give them space again. But there they were still inside him, he discovered, just waiting their chance to jump on him and either paralyse him or urge him to make fundamentally stupid decisions...

Zenas breathed in deep, a wary eye on Jax, who was visibly pale and stressed. 'A diplomatic limousine with a foreign flag drew up. An Arab man in a suit and a crowd of heavies got out. The man had diplomatic credentials but he spoke neither Greek nor English and was unwilling to engage with my questions. Your wife opened the door with your daughter in her arms. She had a stack of suitcases waiting in the hall—'

'And you just let her *go*...?' Jax repeated incredulously. 'You let a bunch of foreigners *kidnap*—'

'She wasn't kidnapped. She went of her own free will,' Zenas told him apologetically. 'We followed the car to the airport where the whole party proceeded through VIP diplomatic channels to which we were denied access. From what we can establish a private jet flew Mrs Antonakos and the little girl to Dharia.'

The name of that country rang a bell of familiarity with Jax. His brow furrowed. There had been some connection. *Thee mou*, his one-time business partner, Rio Benedetti, was married to the sister of the Queen of Dharia...who was coincidentally called... Polly, just like Lucy's long-lost sister. No, he shook away the suspicion until he thought about that slick diplomatic kidnapping—he refused to accept that Lucy had willingly left him—and then the suspicion lodged deep.

Lucy was making a statement, he told himself grimly. He should do nothing and wait for her to get in touch. Lucy would not walk out on him, he told himself. She was annoyed with him. There was nothing he could do about that. He was merely paying the price for having finally told her the truth and if she didn't like the truth, what was he supposed to do about it? Satisfied that he had reached a mature and measured decision, Jax poured himself a stiff drink.

Within the hour he was back pacing the empty marital bedroom. He should not have been imagining Lucy there because they had never yet spent a night in his Athens villa. Yet inexplicably memories of Lucy were everywhere around him. He pictured her on the bed, the softness of her pouty lips, the delicate paleness of her skin, the silky fall of her hair running between his fingers. He snatched in a stark breath. There was a tiny spiralling blonde hair on the dressing table and the scent of the perfume he had bought her in Mykonos still lingered on the air. The bedding was still creased from where she had sat while they'd talked that very afternoon.

Talked? Well, she hadn't really talked, he acknowledged tardily, indeed had been remarkably quiet for a chatterbox. With hindsight it became clear to Jax that she had been upset, *seriously* upset. And he hadn't picked up on that. How could he *not* have picked up on that?

Still locked in the mindset he had had for two long years, Jax had continued to feel like the victim of her treachery. But what if there had been no betrayal in the first place? What if that ridiculous story about sharing clothes was genuine? What if he had abandoned her in Spain two years earlier without any excuse for doing so? And what if he had blown up his marriage over a stupid red dress and a mind-less need to finally confront Lucy?

Jax paced, feeling in dire need of another drink but knowing he shouldn't have one when his brain was already leapfrogging all over the place. Lucy and Bella were gone and he could live with that, couldn't he? A divorce, shared custody, parental access...?

Suddenly feeling very short of breath, Jax froze. There was a tightness in his chest and a dryness in his throat and his heart was thundering in his ears. No, he couldn't live with that option, he decided with dizzy abruptness.

And as so often before when life challenged Jax, anger came to his rescue. He wasn't letting the queen of some tinpot country steal his wife and child! Lucy had been lured away from him and misled and he was going to get her back pronto where she belonged, which was in Greece with him.

'By the sound of it, Jax really doesn't know how to deal with the emotional stuff,' Ellie remarked with a wry smile on her lips.

'That's an understatement,' Polly inputted with a sniff. 'That alley business...accusing her of *that*—'

Ellie laughed and Lucy looked at her red-headed sister in surprise. 'But don't you see? It was all still as fresh as yesterday for Jax, which tells you that he never got over it. Two years on he's still agonising over that alley…yet he still decides to *stay* married to you, he takes you on a honeymoon, acts happy, treats you decently in every other way. It took the equivalent of torture to get the story about the alley out of him because he's *ashamed* that he still wants you, regardless of what he supposedly thinks you did. No, really, Lucy…you can learn a lot from reading between the lines.'

Lucy smiled at that more optimistic viewpoint even if she didn't quite believe in it. She coiled back into her comfortable corner of the sofa in the beautiful room with its impossibly high domed ceiling and wished that she could see what Ellie appeared to see in Jax's behaviour. Her two sisters were so different. Polly was warm and caring, almost motherly, while Ellie was very clever and sympathetic and their children, *her* nephews and nieces, she noted with pleasure, were simply gorgeous.

Polly's boys, Karim and Hassan and Ellie's daughter, Teresina were playing out in the shaded courtyard on trikes. Ellie was feeding her baby boy, Olly, with a bottle while Polly was nursing her newborn daughter, Haifa. Bella was watching the older children scoot around on their bikes while chasing a ball. Karim got off his bike simply to move Bella back a little with her toys, looking out for the toddler in the most considerate way for a small boy.

Lucy was shaken to admit that she would have

been crazily happy in her sister's gorgeous royal palace were it not for Jax's absence. The discovery that her eldest sister was a ruling queen with her husband, Rashad, and that Ellie was the working wife of a fabulously wealthy Italian had certainly helped to take Lucy's mind off her own problems. The three women had sat up into the early hours the first night they were all together, exchanging histories, talking about the three rings they had inherited and catching up on a lifetime of different experiences.

Talking about Jax had come later and had sent Lucy's mood plummeting again because, even though she still felt that walking out on Jax had been the only thing she could do, there was a hollow place inside her where her heart had been ripped out.

In the back of her mind lurked the conviction that Jax had been hurt so much in life just like herself yet they dealt with emotions in very different ways. Jax buried his, hid troubling issues and lived in virtual denial of his feelings. Lucy wore everything on the surface and picked herself up again emotionally no matter how often she was kicked. But she hadn't reacted that way at her last encounter with Jax, she acknowledged. He had hurt her too much and for the first time ever with Jax she had hidden her feelings as well.

In a sense that had been cruel of her and hitting him over the head with something large and heavy might have been kinder. Feelings had to be shoved in Jax's face like placards for him to read them. He had probably been very shocked by her departure and he was probably furious that she had taken their daughter with her. But he still wouldn't understand *why* she had left, which bothered her. The truth was all that had mattered to Jax and he had finally told it without grasping the damage he was doing. He had expected her to excuse him for past events soured by their fathers' machinations. He had not been capable of realising that she had been devastated because everything he had said had spelled out the message that he had never loved, respected or even understood her. How could she possibly love someone like that?

'He's a man. He might as well be from another planet,' Ellie mocked quietly. 'Rio was exactly the same, hiding things, holding onto the past—'

'Rashad too,' Polly admitted ruefully. 'So, perhaps Jax *could* be rehabilitated...'

Lucy studied her linked hands, unable to imagine Jax budging a stubborn inch from his own convictions.

The door opened, framing Rashad, the King of Dharia. Tall and very handsome, he flashed a smile at his wife. 'Polly...we have a visitor. He thinks we kidnapped his wife. What would you have to say to that?'

'Lucy's my sister and I didn't kidnap her... I offered her sanctuary,' Polly declared loftily.

'Sanctuary?' Rashad echoed, visibly appreciating

that choice of word. 'I don't think I would employ that particular word with Jax, Lucy.'

'Jax is here?' Lucy flew off the sofa as though jet-propelled and then stilled, colour rising in her cheeks below her sisters' interested scrutiny.

'Let the rehabilitation commence,' Ellie remarked softly.

'*Have* I been interfering?' Polly asked worriedly.

'No, I was hugely grateful for the support,' Lucy told her warmly.

Lucy couldn't think straight. It had taken Jax less than forty-eight hours to come out to Dharia and she was sharply disconcerted. In the back of her mind, she had feared that he would let her go and write off their marriage as a mistake. After all, how could he possibly *want* to stay married to a woman whom he had such a low opinion of? But then letting her go could well be what he had arrived to discuss, she reasoned unhappily.

Jax was in no better mood after his long flight to find himself in a room decorated like something out of an Arabian Nights' fantasy, which dovetailed beautifully with the royal palace of Dharia. Rashad, the King, had seemed fairly normal though, acknowledging that he too would have been very 'put out' to find his wife and child had staged a vanishing act.

And then Rashad had murmured, 'But now that you're part of the family I should warn you that when the sisters get together, they plot and plan. You're either with them *or* against them.'

'You're my brother-in-law...well, *half*-brother-in-law,' Jax adjusted, recognising that the three sisters had all had different fathers.

'They don't think of each other as half anything,' Rashad cautioned him.

'Catching up?' another voice interposed, a voice that Jax recognised and he tensed, slowly turning round to arrange his thoughts before meeting the eyes of his former business partner, Rio Benedetti. 'Well, isn't this a small world?' he breathed uncomfortably.

'Relax,' the Italian billionaire urged. 'I ran into Franca last year and she brought me up to speed on past events. No disrespect to Franca intended, but I had the lucky escape and *you* had—?'

Jax winced. 'I owe you a wholehearted apology for what happened but let's not talk about it,' he retorted wryly of that sobering experience.

'Let's not,' Rio agreed, leaning closer. 'A word of advice though,' he added in a rueful undertone. 'The word "alley" will be etched on your gravestone...'

Momentarily, Jax froze as if a gun had been angled at him and faint colour rose over his sculpted cheekbones. 'Is that so?'

'The sisters don't keep secrets,' Rio imparted. 'Nothing is too sacred to be discussed. Cross one and you cross all three and none of them are batting for you.'

That was information that Jax could well have done without. He knew he had messed up but everyone else knowing how badly he had messed up made him feel worse. He had had forty-eight hours in which to think and he had done more thinking within that forty-eight hours than he had done in all his twenty-nine years. And having reached obvious conclusions, had even decided what to say.

But Jax's prepared speech flew right out of his head when Lucy walked into the suite he was wafted off to. Lucy was wearing a long flowing dress in shades of blue and it fluttered round her as she moved and just seeing her again, just looking at her again, made Jax feel stuff he couldn't suppress any longer.

'I came because…' he began.

Jax looking gorgeous as usual, Lucy was noting, striving to be cool and composed after Ellie had advised her to play hard to get. But she couldn't play hard to get with Jax, which was the crux of her problem where he was concerned: she loved him. She had always loved him and what had been rather insta-love in Spain when she barely knew him had turned into something much deeper and more binding the second time around. Jax might be hopeless at some things, like talking about feelings and paying compliments, but he was very, *very* good at other things.

'Yes…you were saying?' Lucy prompted, striving to take control of their meeting.

Jax raked a deeply frustrated hand through his tousled black hair, green eyes glinting from below black lashes, and her heart jumped. 'I don't know what I was going to say. I had it all planned out but now it's gone. This is all new to me,' he muttered in a sudden surge. 'But the only really important thing I have to say is that I love you and I need you and I want you to come home with me…'

And just like that and with the unexpectedness of an explosion, Jax stole the wind from Lucy's sails. She didn't have time to try and work out how to play hard to get. He took the breath from her lungs and the arguments from her brain because what he had just said was what she felt as if she had been waiting all her life to hear.

'I've never said those words to anyone else,' Jax admitted gruffly as the silence dragged. 'I married you, not because of your father's blackmail, but because somewhere deep down inside me I *wanted* to be married to you. My head was telling me I didn't want to get married but my instincts were pushing me in a very different direction. Is that weird?'

'No…' Lucy almost whispered the word, scared to move, scared to speak lest she interrupt him and stop him speaking.

'My father reminded me that over one two-week period I flew back to Spain five times to see you. My attachment *was* obsessional,' he conceded grudgingly. 'I loved you then but I was afraid to accept that. Possibly when you said it suited me to believe that file and...*the other stuff* there was a shred of truth in that. Love has always been something that hurt and damaged me. I loved my mother, my father, my little sister, my half-brother and years before I met you I fell for a woman, who turned out to be a very troubled alcoholic, whom I had to place in rehab for recovery. I was determined not to get hurt again.'

Lucy nodded like a vigorous little marionette, wanting so badly to reach out to him and hug him and cover him in kisses but knowing it was wiser to let him say what he needed to say to explain the past and the present. 'I can understand that—'

Jax released his breath on a hiss. 'How can you? You keep on caring about people even when they hurt or disappoint you. That's brave—'

'Or plain stupid,' Lucy slotted in wryly. 'That's just me. I tend to look for saving graces in people and stay optimistic but you're a giant pessimist, who always sees the worst possible conclusions.'

'Pretty much,' Jax conceded.

'And thinks the worst,' Lucy added with spirit, thinking about the alley. 'Even if there's no justification for it.'

Carefully avoiding the word Rio had advised him to avoid, Jax straightened his shoulders. 'The alcoholic that I fell for was repeatedly unfaithful to me. She couldn't help herself—she was a mess until rehab. But like my mother before her she conditioned me to distrust women. I'd seen that file. I saw a woman I thought was you and it seemed to fit, it seemed to be exactly the sort of thing that happened to me—I had got in too deep and you weren't who I thought you were—'

'Like with this alcoholic lady? That would be… er… Franca?' Lucy checked. 'Rio told Ellie about her and Ellie told me.'

Jax took on board the second of Rio's warnings. 'Yes, it was Franca. After her I was very wary and cynical with women. I didn't have faith in my own ability to read a woman, to really *know* her and, life being life,' he groaned, 'that meant I screwed up very badly with you. I ran when I should've stayed. I thought I was protecting myself but you had already burned me.'

'Burned you?'

'I never got over you. I kept on thinking about you at random times and reminding myself how bad you were…you know the—?'

'*Alley* stuff?' Lucy enunciated with precision, bright blue eyes gleaming.

'Yes, that,' Jax muttered, desperately keen to move on. 'Obviously I was wrong and I am very sorry that I believed that was you. I just saw the dress and the blonde hair and—'

Lucy moved closer and closed both arms around him. 'It's all right,' she murmured softly because his voice was ragged and too troubled for her to bear without touching him. 'It's all right. I forgive you. You made a mistake. It's over, done and dusted—'

Jax stared down at her with suspiciously bright green eyes. 'I don't deserve you. You probably don't even believe that I love you and that I loved you right from the start and I don't know how to prove it to you.'

But Lucy didn't need any more proof. Jax had wanted to stay married to her even though he believed she had once been unfaithful to him and that spoke volumes on its own. He had loved her warts and all, carefully schooling himself to overlook what any man would have seen as a monumental flaw and betrayal and predictably keeping his thoughts to himself. And then he had come clean and what he had been keeping secret had shocked and distressed her but at the same time it had set both of them free.

'I love you too,' Lucy whispered, planting a fly-away kiss on his freshly shaven jaw line, which was as high as she could reach even on tiptoes. 'So much that when you're not there it hurts.'

Jax carried her hand to his lips and kissed the back of it in the most un-Jax-like tender manner. 'You didn't even leave me a note. I felt sick. I didn't know what to do. I experienced pure panic—'

'I would've phoned eventually,' she confided. 'I

was so upset but you were right to tell me. It all needed to come out for us to deal with it and then put it away again.'

'Your departure in a royal private jet was fairly straightforward when it came to tracking you,' Jax admitted ruefully, and then he gathered her up into his arms with the attitude of a male who couldn't keep his hands off her any longer.

'The bedroom's next door,' Lucy told him helpfully.

'I even told myself I was only marrying you for Bella's benefit,' Jax confessed. 'I lied to myself all the way down the line.'

'I persuaded myself I was only marrying you for our daughter's benefit as well, so you're not the only one.'

'How's Bella reacting to being here?' Jax queried.

'She's got six cousins to watch and loads of toys to steal. She's having a whale of a time.' Lucy laughed, blue eyes sparkling, and Jax looked down at her with his heart in his own eyes and adoration there, a brilliant smile on his lean, darkly handsome features.

'You are a very special woman, Tinker Bell,' Jax declared, settling her down on the bed with that same heartbreaking smile dazzling her. 'And the saddest element of all this is that my father is now going to be battering down our doors for invites.'

Lucy studied him in bewilderment. 'How? *Why?*'

'Heracles is the son of a pig farmer,' Jax told her

with a chuckle. 'Yes, he keeps that little fact well under wraps because he is an enormous snob. When he discovers that your sister is a queen, he will be horribly friendly. He's very easily impressed in that line.'

Lucy shifted an unconcerned shoulder. 'I can live with that. It's not as though either of us can change our fathers. They are what they are but neither of them is going to get the chance to spoil our happiness again.'

'*Can* you be happy with me?' Jax pressed with touching anxiety. 'You do know I'll screw up again. I won't mean to but I will because I won't always get it right—'

'Neither will I,' Lucy pointed out equably as she struggled to get him out of his jacket and tie and then, when he got helpful, embarked on his shirt, spreading her fingers lasciviously across his muscular torso. 'Love is all about making allowances and compromises. We'll get there. Nobody has to be perfect.'

'I think you are. You have a heart as big as any country, *khriso mou*,' Jax told her with a blissful sigh as she knelt over him, cheerfully stripping him.

'And so have you,' Lucy countered, much amused. 'The difference between us is that you put your heart in a cage to keep it safe—'

'And you still worked your way through the bars of my cage,' Jax reminded her appreciatively. 'You've got more power than you realise.'

Lucy let a small hand stray and he arched up against her as if she had pressed a switch and she laughed as he sat up, wound both hands punitively into her hair and kissed her into breathless, leaping excitement. There was no more conversation then. They were both much too involved in sharing their bodies as they had shared their love.

'I suppose we should get up for dinner…or whatever they call it here,' Jax mused hours later. 'I'm being a very rude guest.'

'No, I know my sisters and they know me. They'll have tucked Bella into bed and gone on as normal. There's no pressure, no expectations. Everyone's family here and that's just the way it is. I *love* it, especially because you're here too now,' Lucy confided, tucking a sleepy head into the crux of a strong brown shoulder and dreamily taking in the familiar scent of his skin, soothed by his proximity and the glorious high of knowing herself loved at last.

'I love you,' Jax muttered, easing her closer, marvelling at how easy it had become to say those words that he had refused to think about for so long.

'Love you,' Lucy whispered, dropping off to sleep, because she had lain awake sleepless while they were apart.

And Jax smiled in the darkness, recognising that for the first time in his life he was truly, joyously happy.

* * *

'This place looks amazing,' Polly carolled as she stood in the marble hall of the house on Tifnos and admired the fabulous Christmas decorations and the glittering tree. 'It's wonderful that you have a home big enough to take us all too, so we can get together like this to celebrate.'

'You can thank my father-in-law, Heracles, for that. He built *big*.'

'Was that the little man who kept on bowing to me?' Polly whispered uneasily.

'Yes, that was him, very subdued at being in the royal presence,' Lucy remarked, stifling her amusement.

In the three years Lucy had been married to Jax a great deal had changed. Her father-in-law was a frequent visitor, their children providing a major draw. Lucy had warmed up to Heracles considerably once she'd realised that he genuinely adored children and his grandchildren most of all. Yes, she had had another baby, a little boy called Dmitri, who was almost two years old. Their lengthy unplanned holiday in Dharia after their reconciliation had extended the family. She had enjoyed her second pregnancy much more than the first because she had had Jax by her side and Jax had been scientifically fascinated by every change she had gone through on the road to producing his son. He had shared everything with her and supported her right through the nausea in the early stages to every medical appointment and finally the birth.

During those three years only Lucy's son had been born but Polly was expecting again, freely admitting that she wanted a large family. Ellie had declared that two children would do her nicely but one never knew with Ellie, who could be prone to saying one thing and then quietly doing another. As for Lucy and Jax, they were still young and, while being quite happy with the children they had, they thought that some day they might plan a third child. Ellie had already lectured them hilariously about birth control, pointing out that *two* accidental conceptions was inexcusable, and her audience had only laughed.

Kreon and Iola were regular visitors on the island and Kreon and Heracles politely avoided each other at family gatherings. Her father had faced bankruptcy proceedings the year before and Jax had bought a small business for him and placed him in it, pointing out that Kreon needed to be kept occupied and independent. His kindness had almost reduced Lucy to tears and she was relieved that Jax had finally begun to see and understand Kreon's essential good-heartedness.

'He's your father and you love him,' Jax had said to Lucy. 'We have to do our best for him. After all, you put up with my father and forgive his foibles.'

Jax was a wonderful husband in every way, Lucy reflected gratefully, feeling very blessed. After spending so many years of craving the feeling of being special to someone she had finally found a safe harbour.

Leaving Polly to get settled in with her children and explaining that Ellie had gone straight to bed after a hospital late night shift, Lucy went off to put Dmitri down for a nap because he got very cross and whiny when he got too tired and with all the children in the house and the excitement of the Christmas season, he needed more sleep. The little boy snuggled into his cot, clutching his toy elephant. He was as blonde as his mother, which had been a surprise to his parents, but he too had Jax's green eyes and olive complexion.

Lucy looked out of the window and saw the older children down on the beach with Rashad and Rio. She could just make out four-year-old Bella in her yellow dress skipping through the surf with Polly's younger son, Hassan, and Ellie's Teresina. The cousins had all become fast friends and playmates, which made family get-togethers run more smoothly.

Recognising that she finally had the family circle she had dreamt of having all her life, Lucy vented a contented sigh and went to freshen up before dinner. She was in the shower when another body stepped in beside her and she spun round with a delighted smile of welcome.

'Jax…thought you were going to be late tonight!' she gasped.

'No, I looked round my office, thought of you all here enjoying yourselves without me and decided I was needed at home. I saw the children down on the beach as we flew in.'

'Dmitri's having a nap. He was throwing tantrums all over the place,' his mother confided ruefully.

'I swear he's got my mother's temperament,' Jax said worriedly.

'No, don't be silly,' Lucy soothed, aware that he had that little fear that he might somehow pass on some troublesome gene. 'He's a toddler with a short temper and he hasn't learned to control it yet. When he's not tired he's very good-natured. And, hey, did you join me in the shower to talk about the kids or—?'

'Or, *agapi mou*,' Jax chose, plastering her back against the shower wall and tasting her lush mouth with hungry urgency.

Lucy melted every time he called her his love. He was hot and wet and gorgeous and all hers. Excitement rippled through her in seductive sensual waves.

'Birth control,' Jax growled, lifting her out of the shower and throwing a heap of towels down on the tiled floor as he dug into a drawer for the necessary.

Lucy arranged herself on the towels and giggled like a drain. 'Ellie really got to you with that lecture, didn't she?'

'Ellie knows how to make a man feel irresponsible,' Jax responded. 'And I will *never* be irresponsible with you again but don't tell her that.'

'I promise I won't.' Her amusement dying as they joined, Lucy lifted tender fingers to stroke his jaw line. 'I love you, Jax Antonakos... I love you so much.'

He was too otherwise engaged to speak at that moment but his emerald eyes telegraphed love and passion and need and that was more than sufficient for Lucy, who knew a good man when she found one and held fast to him because he gave her so much happiness.

* * * * *

If you enjoyed the final part of Lynne Graham's
BRIDES FOR THE TAKING *trilogy,*
why not explore the first two instalments?

THE DESERT KING'S BLACKMAILED BRIDE
THE ITALIAN'S ONE-NIGHT BABY

Available now!